THERE WAS IN BAGHDAD THE MAGNIFICENT A GRAND VIZIER (5 FEET TALL IN HIS POINTY SLIPPERS) NAMED IZNOGOUD. HE WAS TRULY NASTY AND HAD ONLY ONE GOAL...

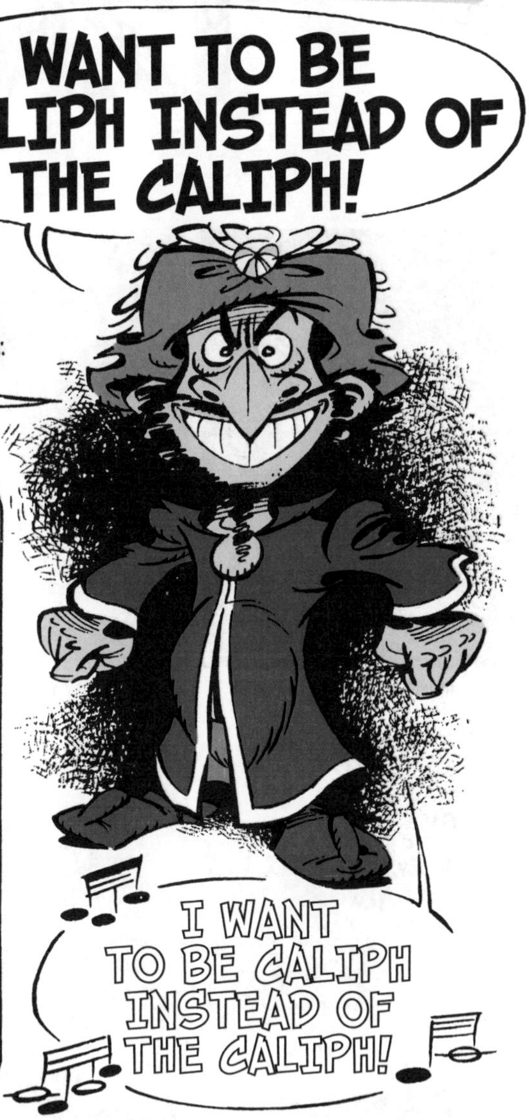
I WANT TO BE CALIPH INSTEAD OF THE CALIPH!
I WANT TO BE CALIPH INSTEAD OF THE CALIPH!
I WANT TO BE CALIPH INSTEAD OF THE CALIPH!

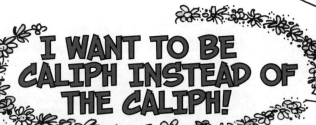

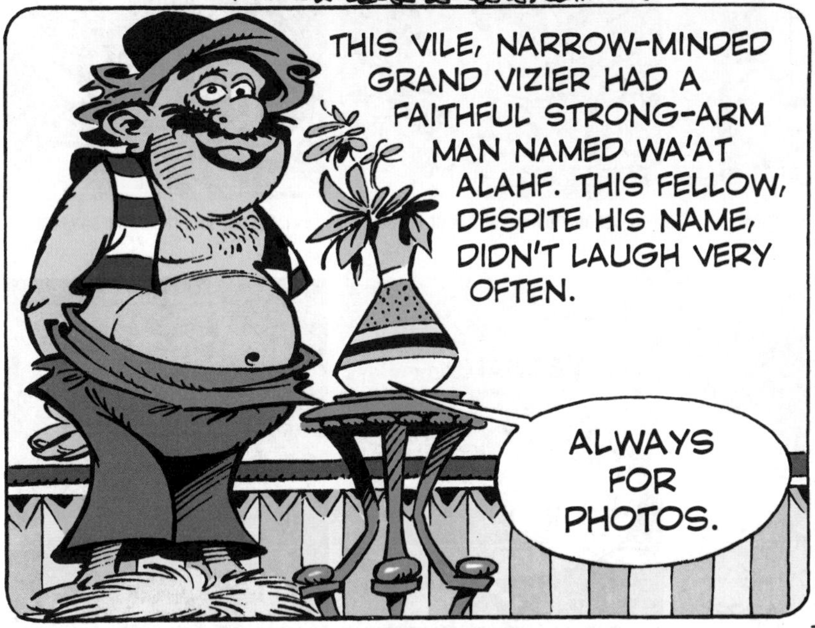
THIS VILE, NARROW-MINDED GRAND VIZIER HAD A FAITHFUL STRONG-ARM MAN NAMED WA'AT ALAHF. THIS FELLOW, DESPITE HIS NAME, DIDN'T LAUGH VERY OFTEN.
ALWAYS FOR PHOTOS.

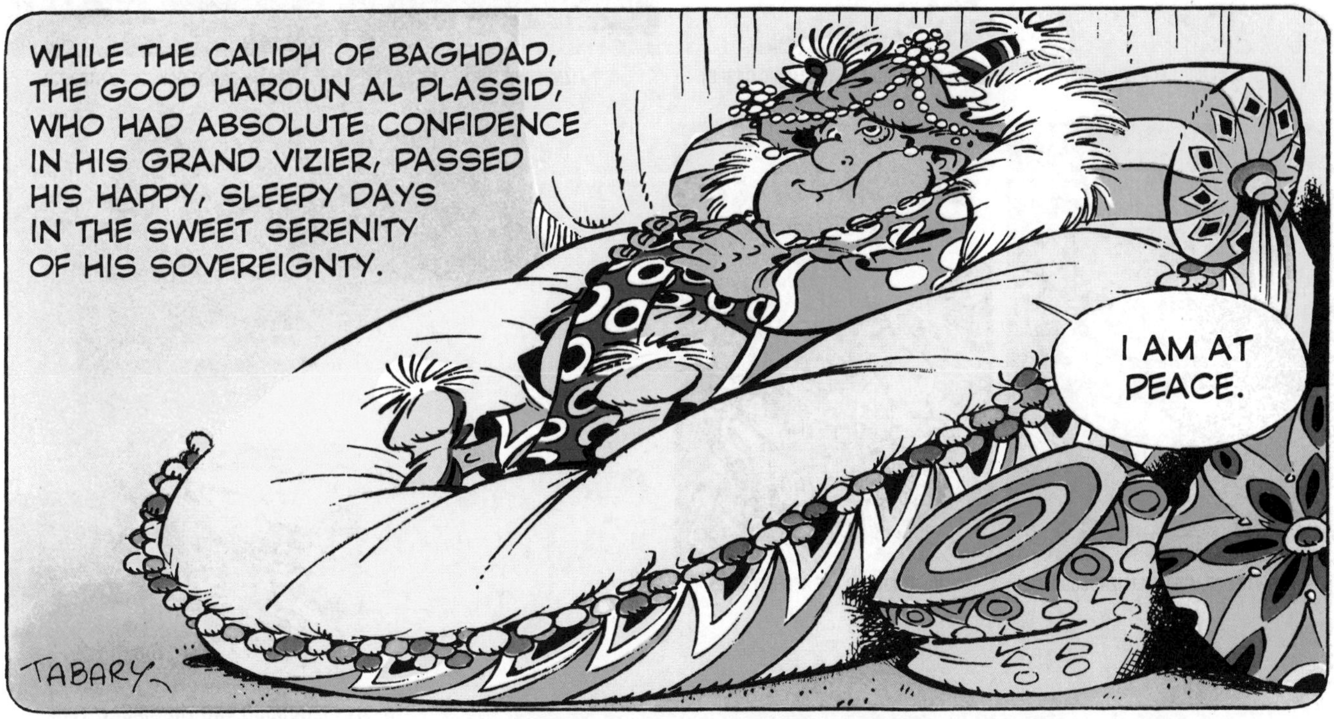
WHILE THE CALIPH OF BAGHDAD, THE GOOD HAROUN AL PLASSID, WHO HAD ABSOLUTE CONFIDENCE IN HIS GRAND VIZIER, PASSED HIS HAPPY, SLEEPY DAYS IN THE SWEET SERENITY OF HIS SOVEREIGNTY.
I AM AT PEACE.
TABARY

NOW THEN, TO BAGHDAD THE MAGNIFICENT...

IZNOGOUD

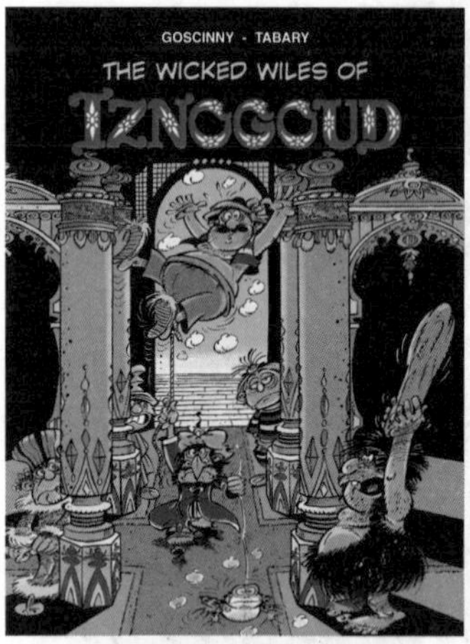
GOSCINNY - TABARY
THE WICKED WILES OF
IZNOGOUD

1 - THE WICKED WILES OF IZNOGOUD

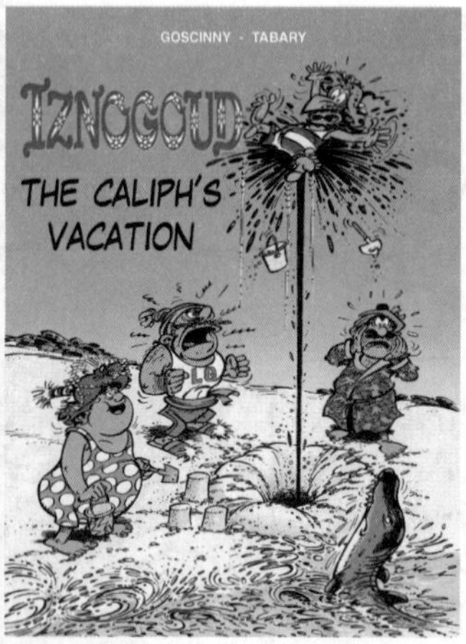
GOSCINNY - TABARY
IZNOGOUD
THE CALIPH'S VACATION

2 - THE CALIPH'S VACATION

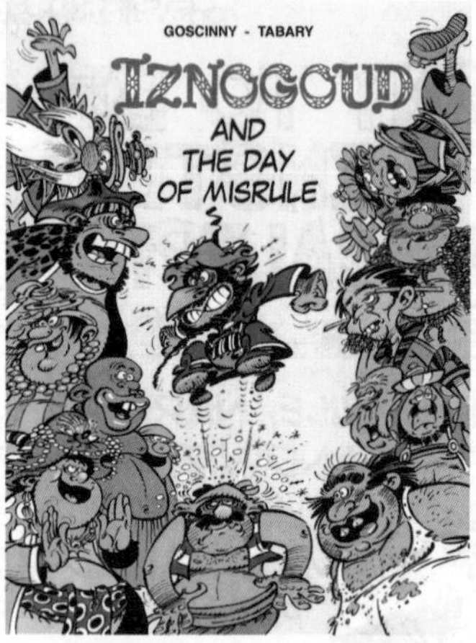
GOSCINNY - TABARY
IZNOGOUD
AND THE DAY OF MISRULE

3 - IZNOGOUD AND THE DAY OF MISRULE

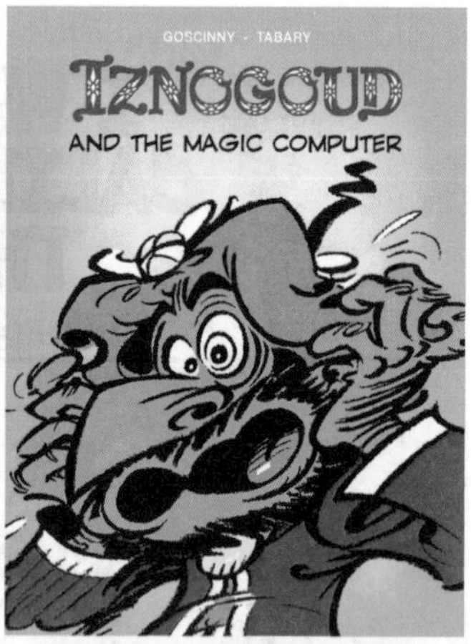
GOSCINNY - TABARY
IZNOGOUD
AND THE MAGIC COMPUTER

4 - IZNOGOUD AND THE MAGIC COMPUTER

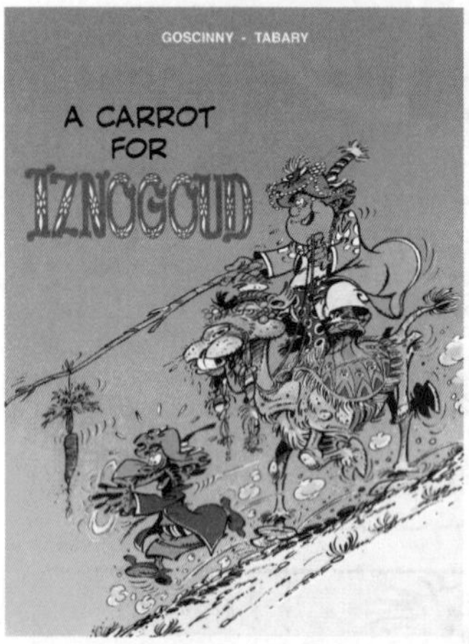
GOSCINNY - TABARY
A CARROT FOR
IZNOGOUD

5 - A CARROT FOR IZNOGOUD

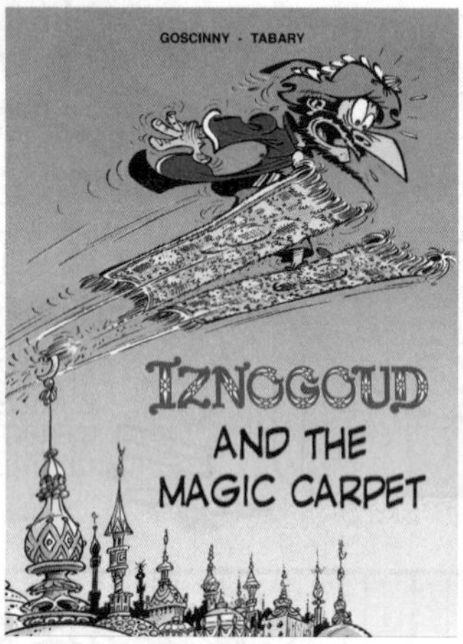
GOSCINNY - TABARY
IZNOGOUD
AND THE MAGIC CARPET

6 - IZNOGOUD AND THE MAGIC CARPET

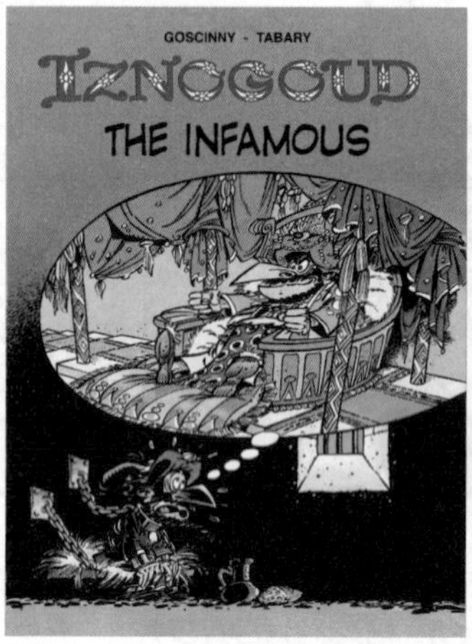
GOSCINNY - TABARY
IZNOGOUD
THE INFAMOUS

7 - IZNOGOUD THE INFAMOUS

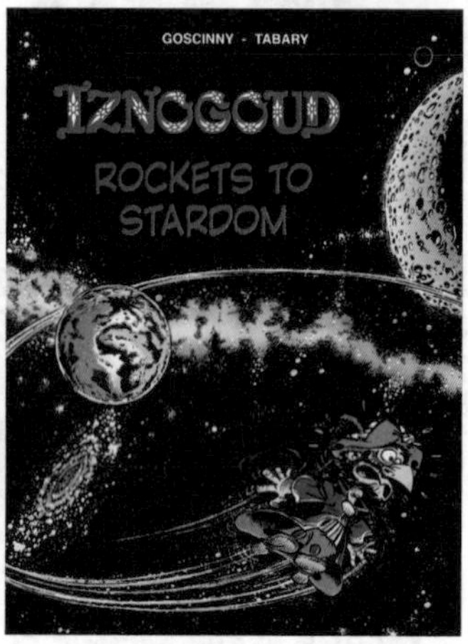
GOSCINNY - TABARY
IZNOGOUD
ROCKETS TO STARDOM

8 - IZNOGOUD ROCKETS TO STARDOM

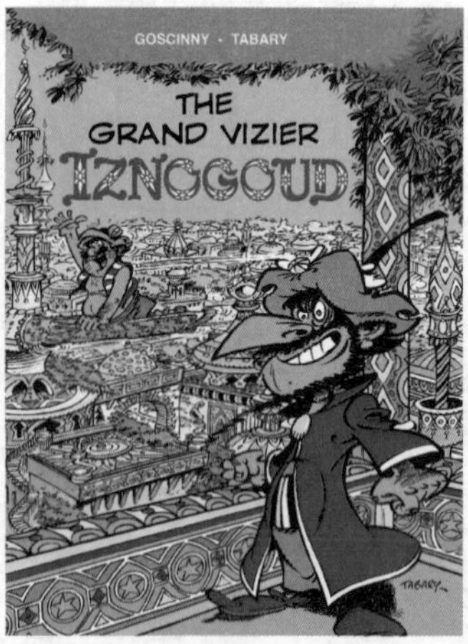
GOSCINNY - TABARY
THE GRAND VIZIER
IZNOGOUD

9 - THE GRAND VIZIER IZNOGOUD

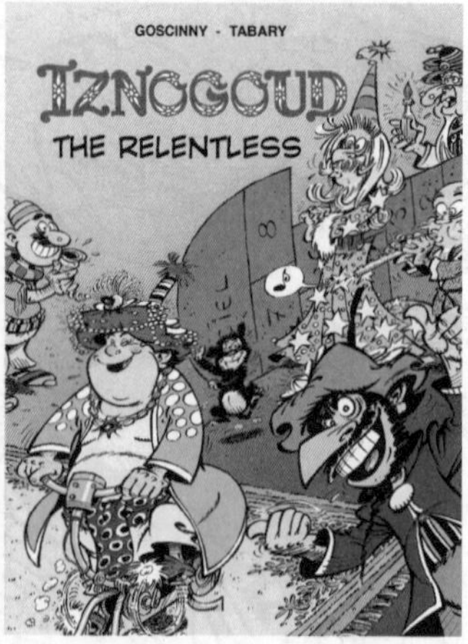
GOSCINNY - TABARY
IZNOGOUD
THE RELENTLESS

10 - IZNOGOUD THE RELENTLESS

COMING SOON

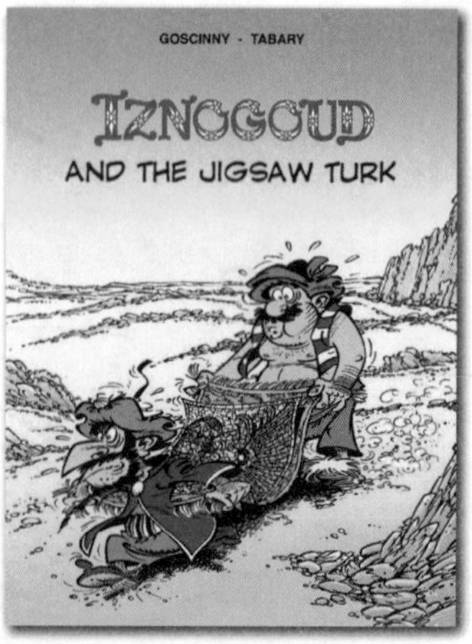
GOSCINNY - TABARY
IZNOGOUD
AND THE JIGSAW TURK

11 - IZNOGOUD AND THE JIGSAW TURK

THE ADVENTURES OF THE GRAND VIZIER IZNOGOUD
BY GOSCINNY & TABARY

IZNOGOUD
THE RELENTLESS

SCRIPT: GOSCINNY   **DRAWING: TABARY**

Original title: Iznogoud l'acharné

Original edition: © 2013 IMAV éditions / Goscinny – Tabary
www.imaveditions.com
www.iznogoud.com
All rights reserved

English translation: © 2013 Cinebook Ltd

Translator: Jerome Saincantin
Lettering and text layout: Design Amorandi
Printed in Spain by Just Colour Graphic

This edition published in Great Britain in 2013 by
Cinebook Ltd
56 Beech Avenue,
Canterbury, Kent
CT4 7TA
www.cinebook.com

A CIP catalogue record for this book
is available from the British Library

ISBN 978-1-84918-181-5

9th CINEBOOK
The 9th Art Publisher

THESE ANONYMOUS CHILDREN, IN A RANDOM COURTYARD OF AN UNKNOWN HOUSE IN SOME TOWN OR OTHER, ARE PLAYING HOPSCOTCH. BUT DID YOU KNOW THAT TO FIND THE ORIGIN OF THIS CHILDISH GAME, WE MUST TRAVEL BACK IN TIME TO THE REIGN OF GOOD HAROUN AL PLASSID, CALIPH OF BAGHDAD? IF YOU DIDN'T, THEN HURRY UP AND READ THIS STORY, WHICH WILL TEACH YOU THE WHOLE, TERRIBLE TRUTH ABOUT...

THE MALEFIC HOPSCOTCH GRID

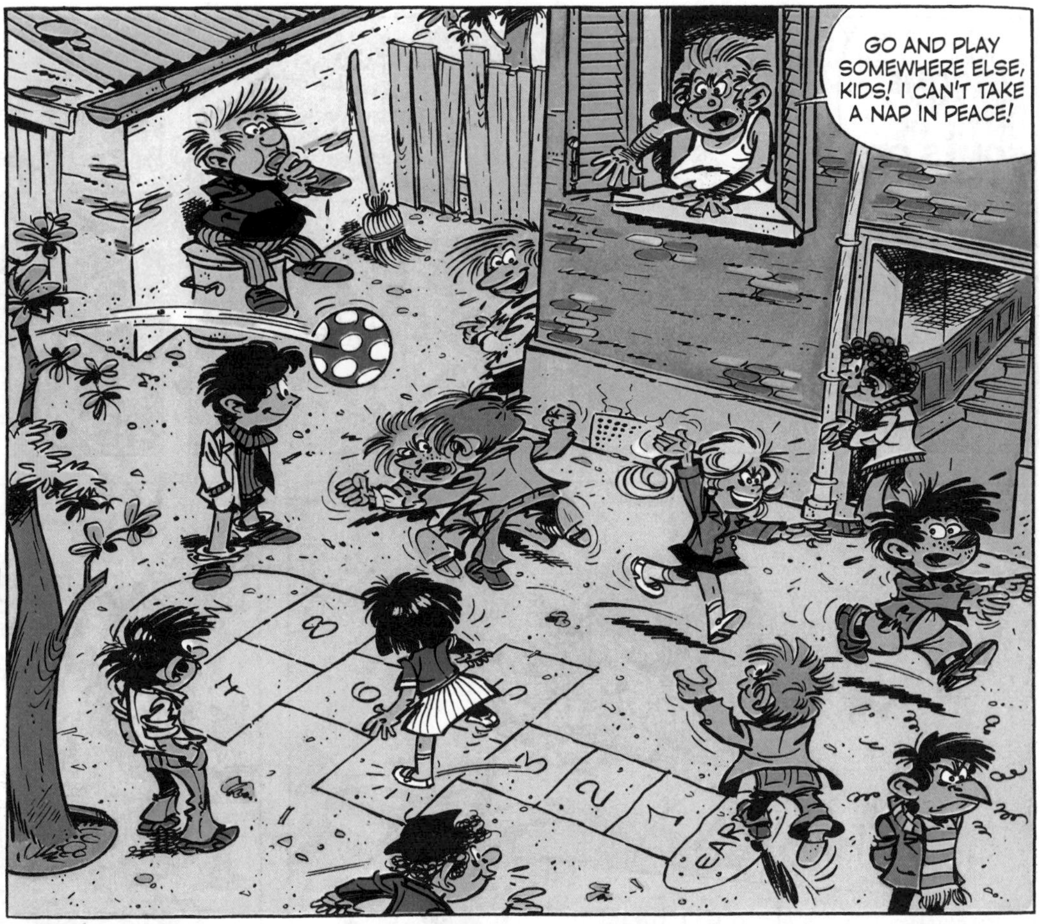
GO AND PLAY SOMEWHERE ELSE, KIDS! I CAN'T TAKE A NAP IN PEACE!

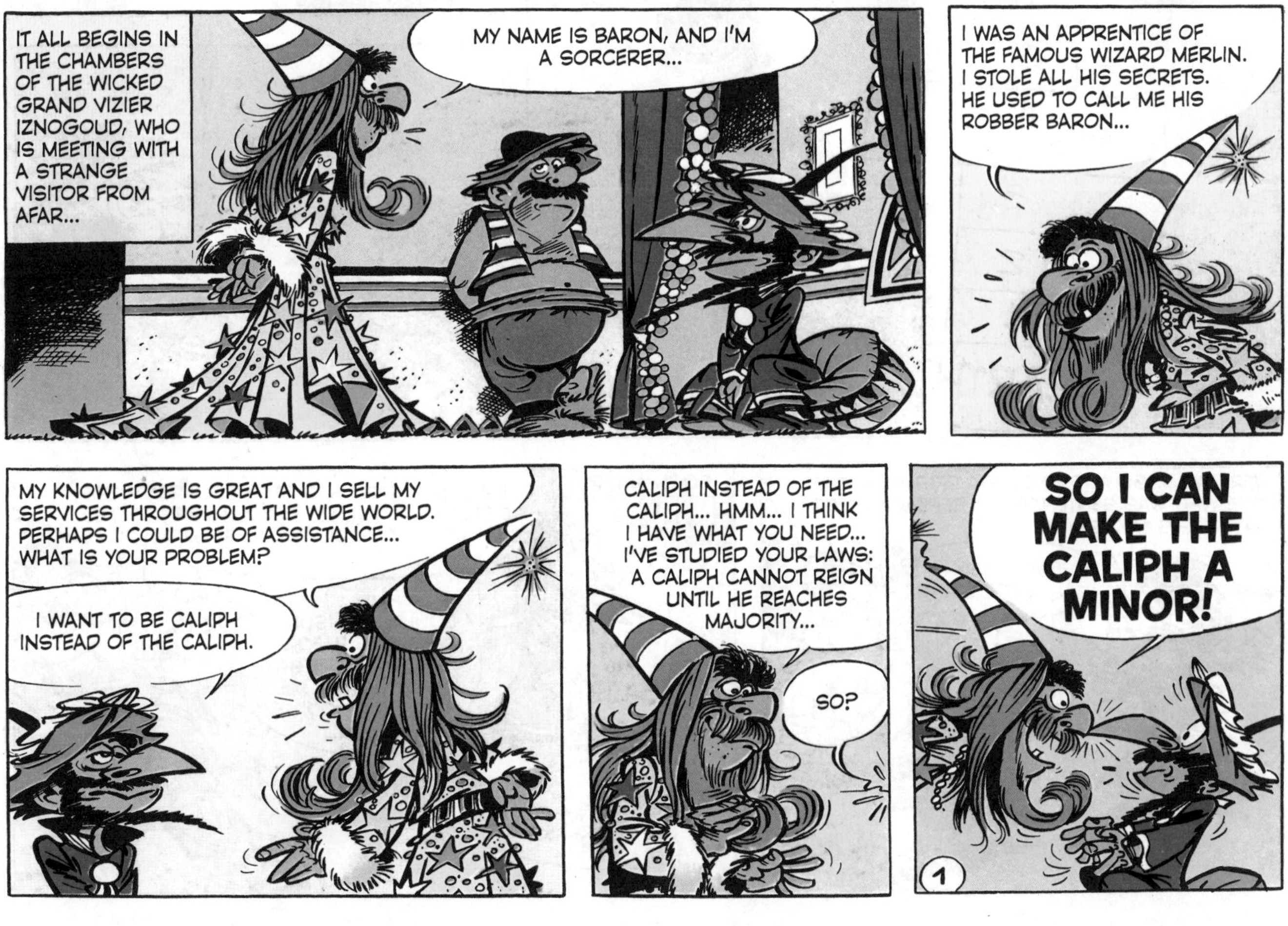
IT ALL BEGINS IN THE CHAMBERS OF THE WICKED GRAND VIZIER IZNOGOUD, WHO IS MEETING WITH A STRANGE VISITOR FROM AFAR...
MY NAME IS BARON, AND I'M A SORCERER...
I WAS AN APPRENTICE OF THE FAMOUS WIZARD MERLIN. I STOLE ALL HIS SECRETS. HE USED TO CALL ME HIS ROBBER BARON...
MY KNOWLEDGE IS GREAT AND I SELL MY SERVICES THROUGHOUT THE WIDE WORLD. PERHAPS I COULD BE OF ASSISTANCE... WHAT IS YOUR PROBLEM?
I WANT TO BE CALIPH INSTEAD OF THE CALIPH.
CALIPH INSTEAD OF THE CALIPH... HMM... I THINK I HAVE WHAT YOU NEED... I'VE STUDIED YOUR LAWS: A CALIPH CANNOT REIGN UNTIL HE REACHES MAJORITY...
SO?
SO I CAN MAKE THE CALIPH A MINOR!
1

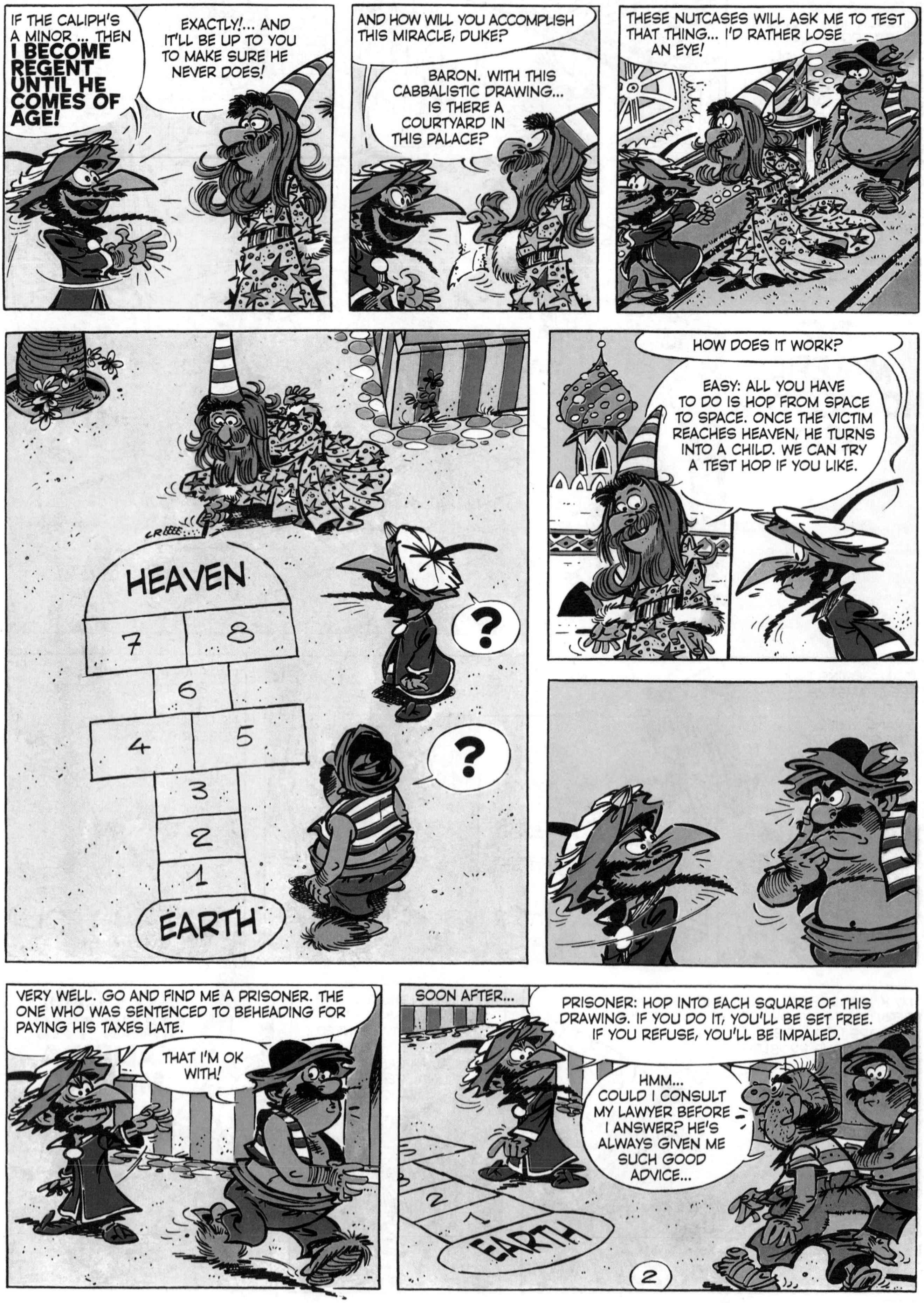
IF THE CALIPH'S A MINOR ... THEN I BECOME REGENT UNTIL HE COMES OF AGE!
EXACTLY!... AND IT'LL BE UP TO YOU TO MAKE SURE HE NEVER DOES!
AND HOW WILL YOU ACCOMPLISH THIS MIRACLE, DUKE?
BARON. WITH THIS CABBALISTIC DRAWING... IS THERE A COURTYARD IN THIS PALACE?
THESE NUTCASES WILL ASK ME TO TEST THAT THING... I'D RATHER LOSE AN EYE!
CREEE
HEAVEN
7
8
6
4
5
3
2
1
EARTH
?
?
HOW DOES IT WORK?
EASY: ALL YOU HAVE TO DO IS HOP FROM SPACE TO SPACE. ONCE THE VICTIM REACHES HEAVEN, HE TURNS INTO A CHILD. WE CAN TRY A TEST HOP IF YOU LIKE.
VERY WELL. GO AND FIND ME A PRISONER. THE ONE WHO WAS SENTENCED TO BEHEADING FOR PAYING HIS TAXES LATE.
THAT I'M OK WITH!
SOON AFTER...
PRISONER: HOP INTO EACH SQUARE OF THIS DRAWING. IF YOU DO IT, YOU'LL BE SET FREE. IF YOU REFUSE, YOU'LL BE IMPALED.
HMM... COULD I CONSULT MY LAWYER BEFORE I ANSWER? HE'S ALWAYS GIVEN ME SUCH GOOD ADVICE...
2
1
EARTH
2

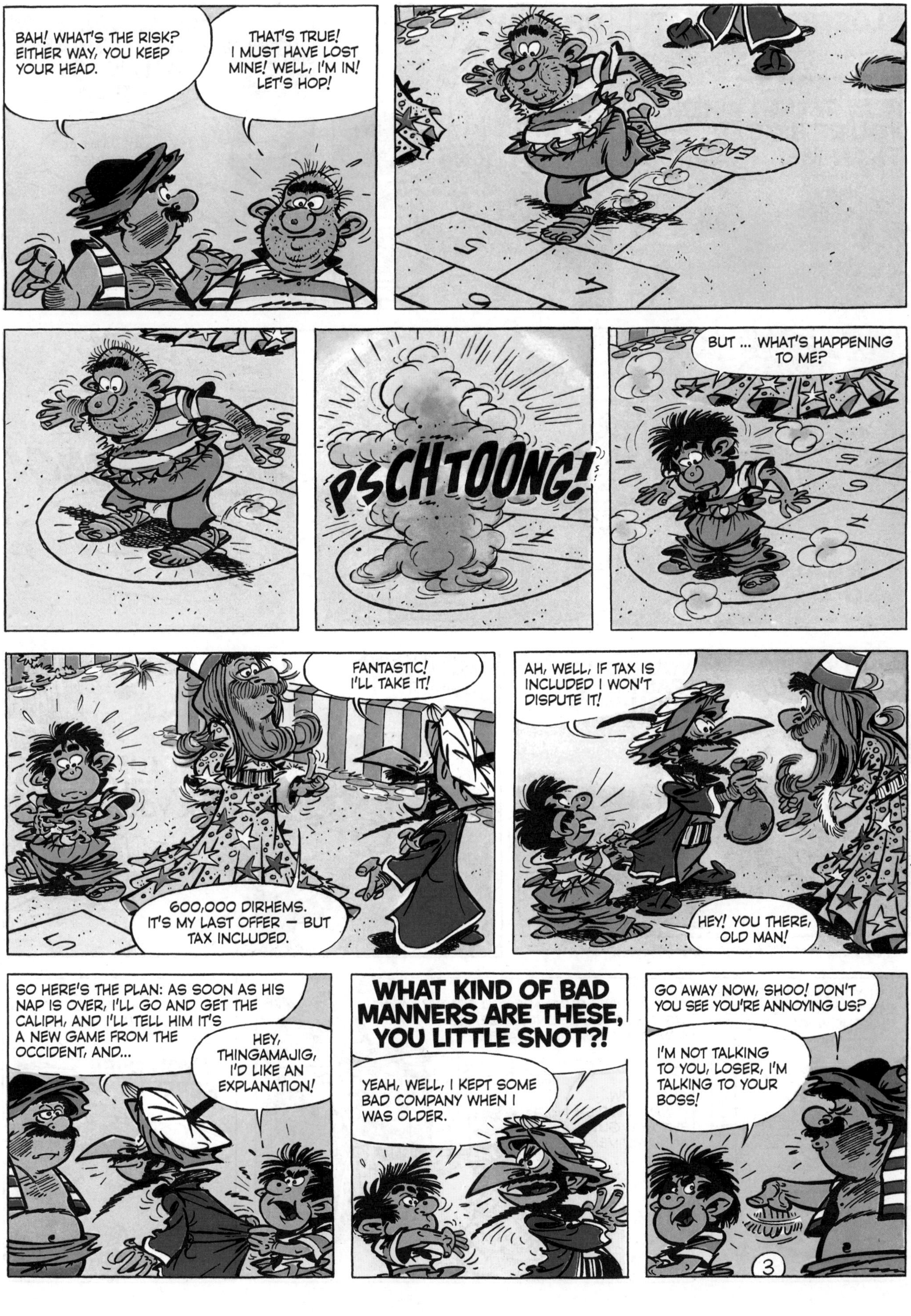
BAH! WHAT'S THE RISK? EITHER WAY, YOU KEEP YOUR HEAD.
THAT'S TRUE! I MUST HAVE LOST MINE! WELL, I'M IN! LET'S HOP!
EARTH
5
4
6
PSCHTOONG!
BUT ... WHAT'S HAPPENING TO ME?
FANTASTIC! I'LL TAKE IT!
600,000 DIRHEMS. IT'S MY LAST OFFER — BUT TAX INCLUDED.
AH, WELL, IF TAX IS INCLUDED I WON'T DISPUTE IT!
HEY! YOU THERE, OLD MAN!
SO HERE'S THE PLAN: AS SOON AS HIS NAP IS OVER, I'LL GO AND GET THE CALIPH, AND I'LL TELL HIM IT'S A NEW GAME FROM THE OCCIDENT, AND...
HEY, THINGAMAJIG, I'D LIKE AN EXPLANATION!
WHAT KIND OF BAD MANNERS ARE THESE, YOU LITTLE SNOT?!
YEAH, WELL, I KEPT SOME BAD COMPANY WHEN I WAS OLDER.
GO AWAY NOW, SHOO! DON'T YOU SEE YOU'RE ANNOYING US?
I'M NOT TALKING TO YOU, LOSER, I'M TALKING TO YOUR BOSS!
3

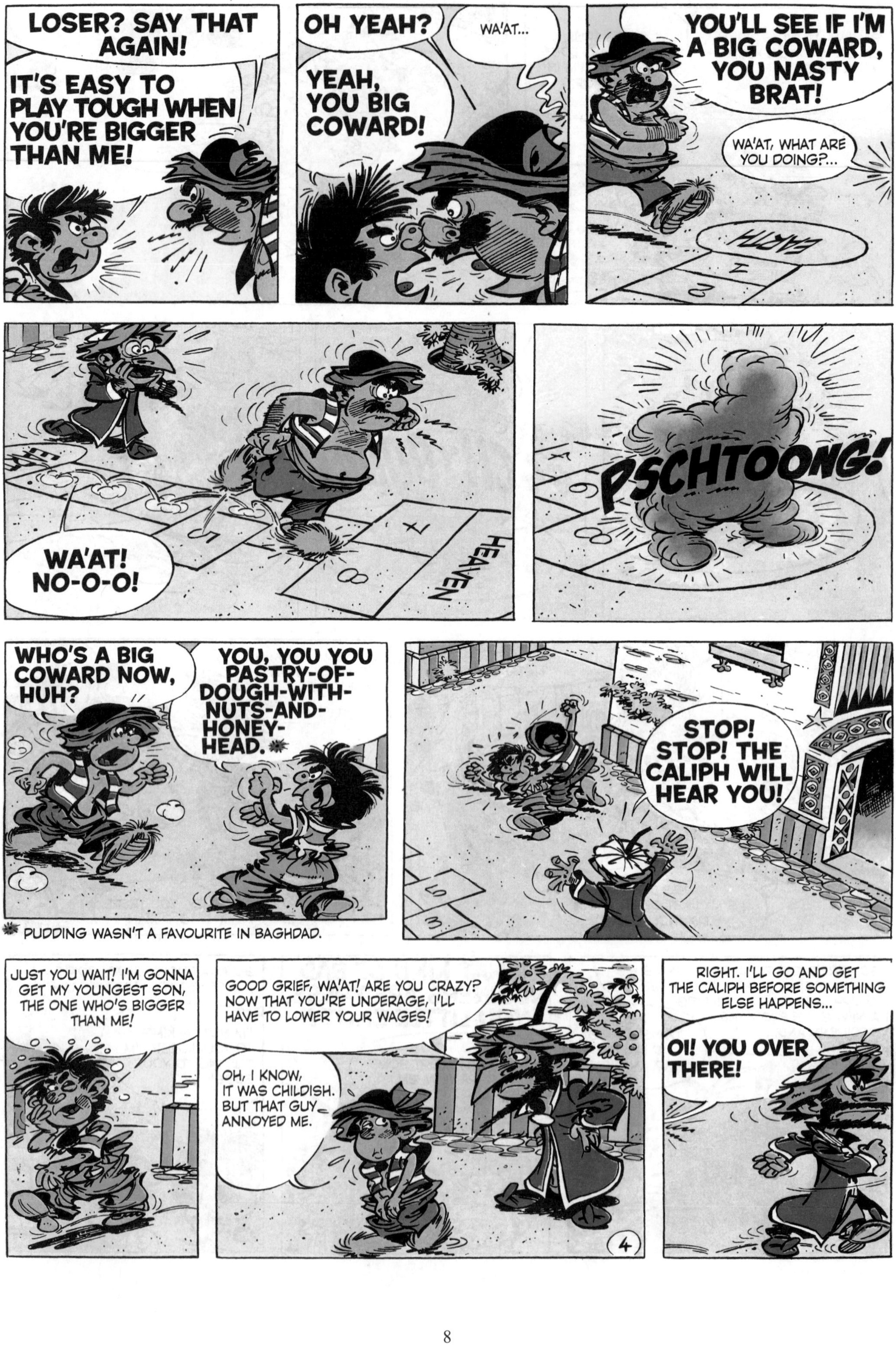
LOSER? SAY THAT AGAIN!
IT'S EASY TO PLAY TOUGH WHEN YOU'RE BIGGER THAN ME!
OH YEAH?
WA'AT...
YEAH, YOU BIG COWARD!
YOU'LL SEE IF I'M A BIG COWARD, YOU NASTY BRAT!
WA'AT, WHAT ARE YOU DOING?...
WA'AT! NO-O-O!
HEAVEN
PSCHTOONG!
WHO'S A BIG COWARD NOW, HUH?
YOU, YOU YOU PASTRY-OF-DOUGH-WITH-NUTS-AND-HONEY-HEAD.*
STOP! STOP! THE CALIPH WILL HEAR YOU!
JUST YOU WAIT! I'M GONNA GET MY YOUNGEST SON, THE ONE WHO'S BIGGER THAN ME!
GOOD GRIEF, WA'AT! ARE YOU CRAZY? NOW THAT YOU'RE UNDERAGE, I'LL HAVE TO LOWER YOUR WAGES!
OH, I KNOW, IT WAS CHILDISH. BUT THAT GUY ANNOYED ME.
RIGHT. I'LL GO AND GET THE CALIPH BEFORE SOMETHING ELSE HAPPENS...
OI! YOU OVER THERE!

* PUDDING WASN'T A FAVOURITE IN BAGHDAD.

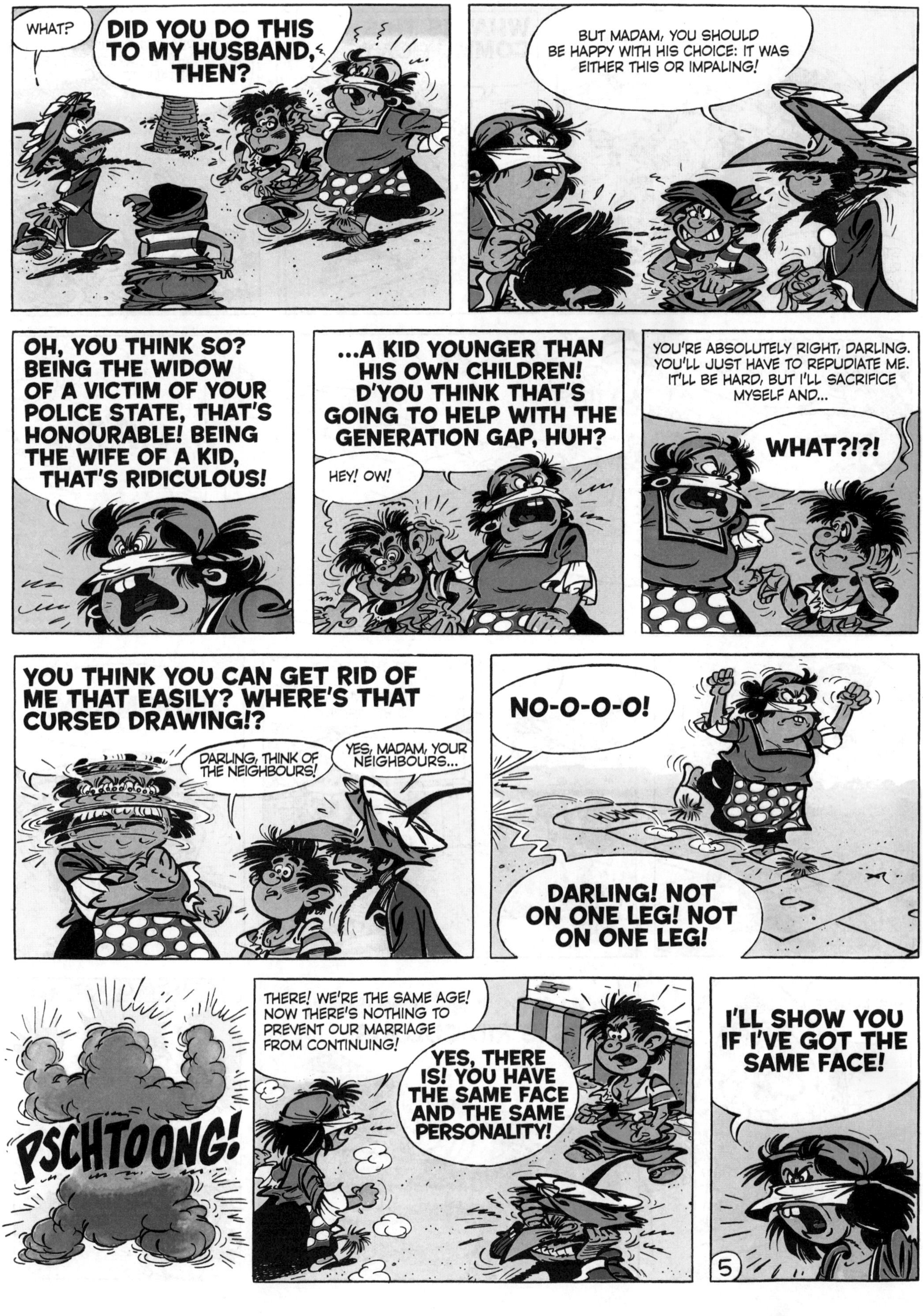
WHAT?
DID YOU DO THIS TO MY HUSBAND, THEN?
BUT MADAM, YOU SHOULD BE HAPPY WITH HIS CHOICE: IT WAS EITHER THIS OR IMPALING!
OH, YOU THINK SO? BEING THE WIDOW OF A VICTIM OF YOUR POLICE STATE, THAT'S HONOURABLE! BEING THE WIFE OF A KID, THAT'S RIDICULOUS!
...A KID YOUNGER THAN HIS OWN CHILDREN! D'YOU THINK THAT'S GOING TO HELP WITH THE GENERATION GAP, HUH?
HEY! OW!
YOU'RE ABSOLUTELY RIGHT, DARLING. YOU'LL JUST HAVE TO REPUDIATE ME. IT'LL BE HARD, BUT I'LL SACRIFICE MYSELF AND...
WHAT?!?!
YOU THINK YOU CAN GET RID OF ME THAT EASILY? WHERE'S THAT CURSED DRAWING!?
DARLING, THINK OF THE NEIGHBOURS!
YES, MADAM, YOUR NEIGHBOURS...
NO-O-O-O!
DARLING! NOT ON ONE LEG! NOT ON ONE LEG!
PSCHTOONG!
THERE! WE'RE THE SAME AGE! NOW THERE'S NOTHING TO PREVENT OUR MARRIAGE FROM CONTINUING!
YES, THERE IS! YOU HAVE THE SAME FACE AND THE SAME PERSONALITY!
I'LL SHOW YOU IF I'VE GOT THE SAME FACE!
5

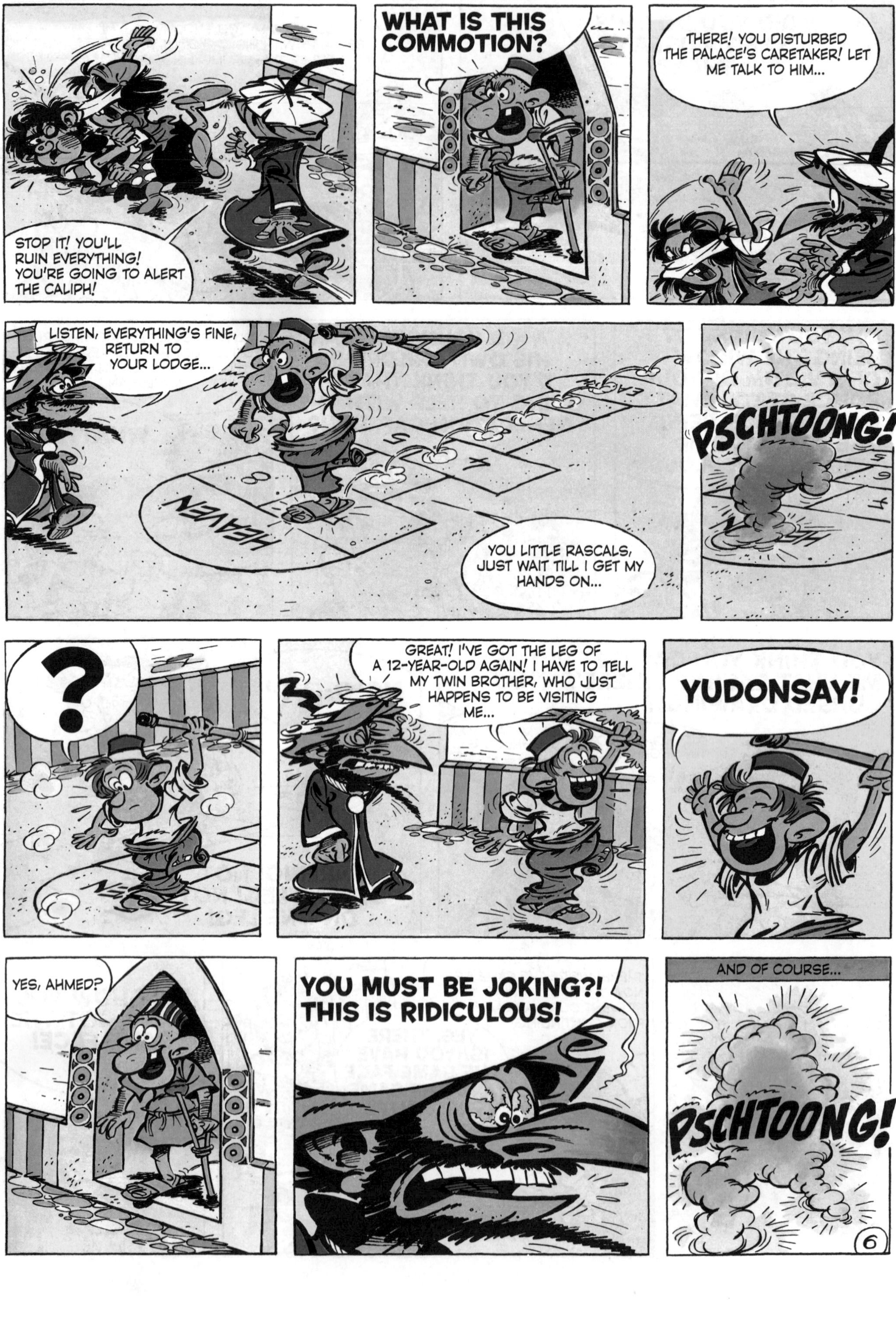
STOP IT! YOU'LL RUIN EVERYTHING! YOU'RE GOING TO ALERT THE CALIPH!
WHAT IS THIS COMMOTION?
THERE! YOU DISTURBED THE PALACE'S CARETAKER! LET ME TALK TO HIM...
LISTEN, EVERYTHING'S FINE, RETURN TO YOUR LODGE...
HEAVEN
EARTH
YOU LITTLE RASCALS, JUST WAIT TILL I GET MY HANDS ON...
PSCHTOONG!
?
GREAT! I'VE GOT THE LEG OF A 12-YEAR-OLD AGAIN! I HAVE TO TELL MY TWIN BROTHER, WHO JUST HAPPENS TO BE VISITING ME...
YUDONSAY!
YES, AHMED?
YOU MUST BE JOKING?! THIS IS RIDICULOUS!
AND OF COURSE...
PSCHTOONG!
6

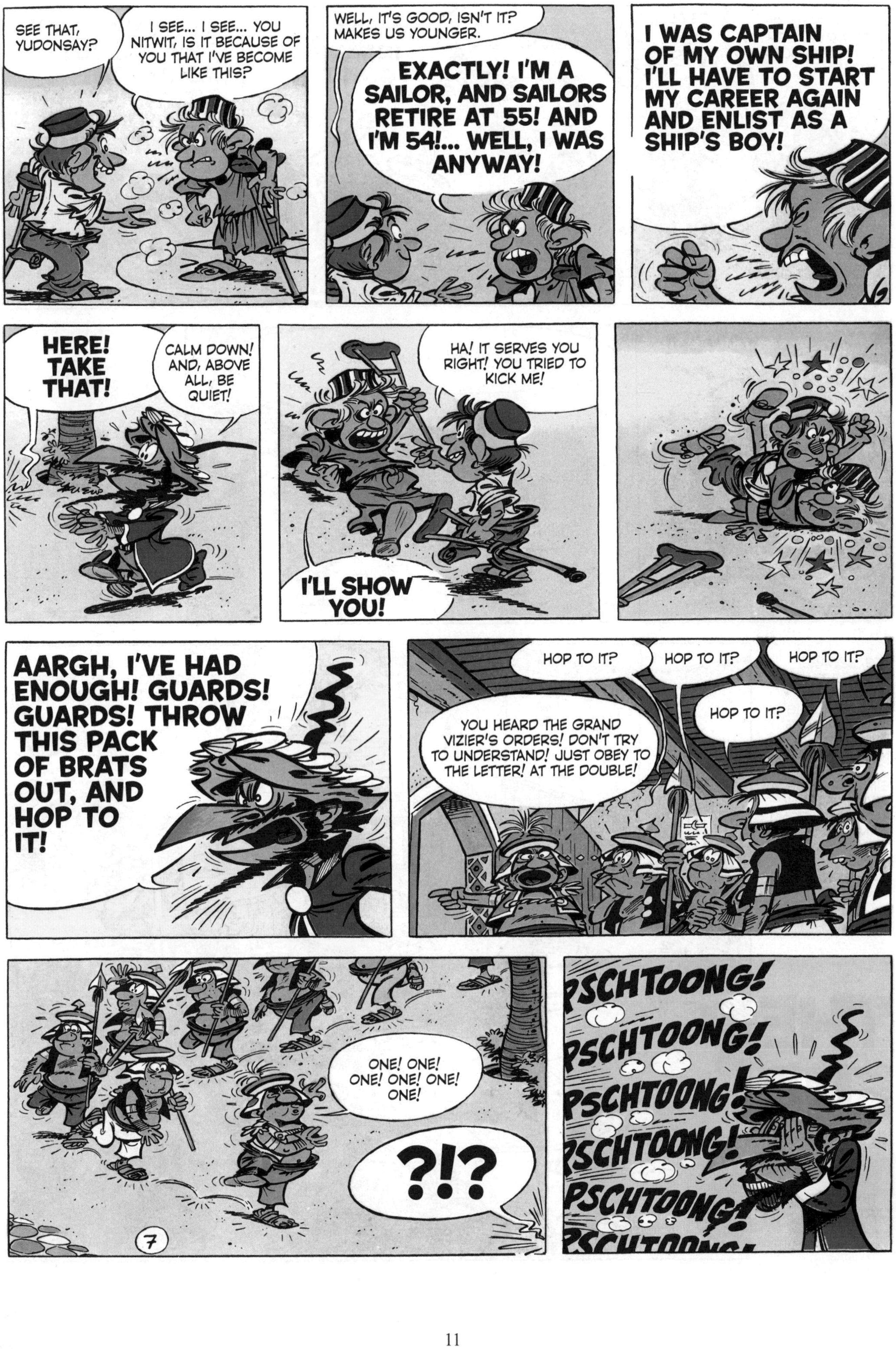
SEE THAT, YUDONSAY?
I SEE... I SEE... YOU NITWIT, IS IT BECAUSE OF YOU THAT I'VE BECOME LIKE THIS?
WELL, IT'S GOOD, ISN'T IT? MAKES US YOUNGER.
EXACTLY! I'M A SAILOR, AND SAILORS RETIRE AT 55! AND I'M 54!... WELL, I WAS ANYWAY!
I WAS CAPTAIN OF MY OWN SHIP! I'LL HAVE TO START MY CAREER AGAIN AND ENLIST AS A SHIP'S BOY!
HERE! TAKE THAT!
CALM DOWN! AND, ABOVE ALL, BE QUIET!
HA! IT SERVES YOU RIGHT! YOU TRIED TO KICK ME!
I'LL SHOW YOU!
AARGH, I'VE HAD ENOUGH! GUARDS! GUARDS! THROW THIS PACK OF BRATS OUT, AND HOP TO IT!
HOP TO IT?
HOP TO IT?
HOP TO IT?
HOP TO IT?
YOU HEARD THE GRAND VIZIER'S ORDERS! DON'T TRY TO UNDERSTAND! JUST OBEY TO THE LETTER! AT THE DOUBLE!
ONE! ONE! ONE! ONE! ONE! ONE!
?!?
7
PSCHTOONG!
PSCHTOONG!
PSCHTOONG!
PSCHTOONG!
PSCHTOONG!

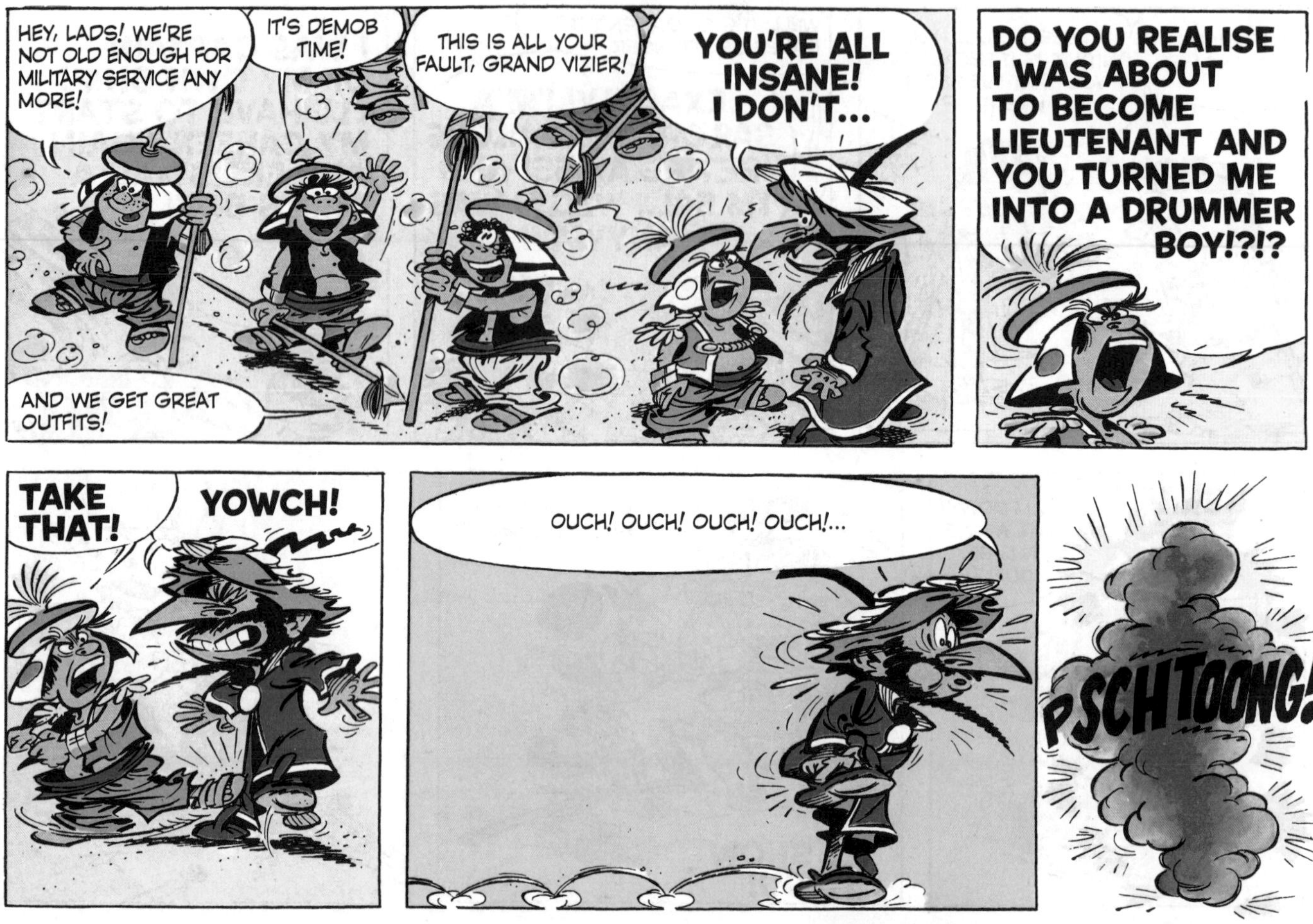
HEY, LADS! WE'RE NOT OLD ENOUGH FOR MILITARY SERVICE ANY MORE!
AND WE GET GREAT OUTFITS!
IT'S DEMOB TIME!
THIS IS ALL YOUR FAULT, GRAND VIZIER!
YOU'RE ALL INSANE! I DON'T...
DO YOU REALISE I WAS ABOUT TO BECOME LIEUTENANT AND YOU TURNED ME INTO A DRUMMER BOY!?!?
TAKE THAT!
YOWCH!
OUCH! OUCH! OUCH! OUCH!...
PSCHTOONG!

YES, BEWARE HOPSCOTCH; HARMLESS TO CHILDREN, IT IS EVIL TO ADULTS! YOU WHO ARE NOW OVER FORTY, IF YOU SEE THAT SINISTER MYSTICAL DRAWING, RUN! RUN IF YOU DON'T WANT TO LOSE ALL THE ADVANTAGES OF GLORIOUS MATURITY!

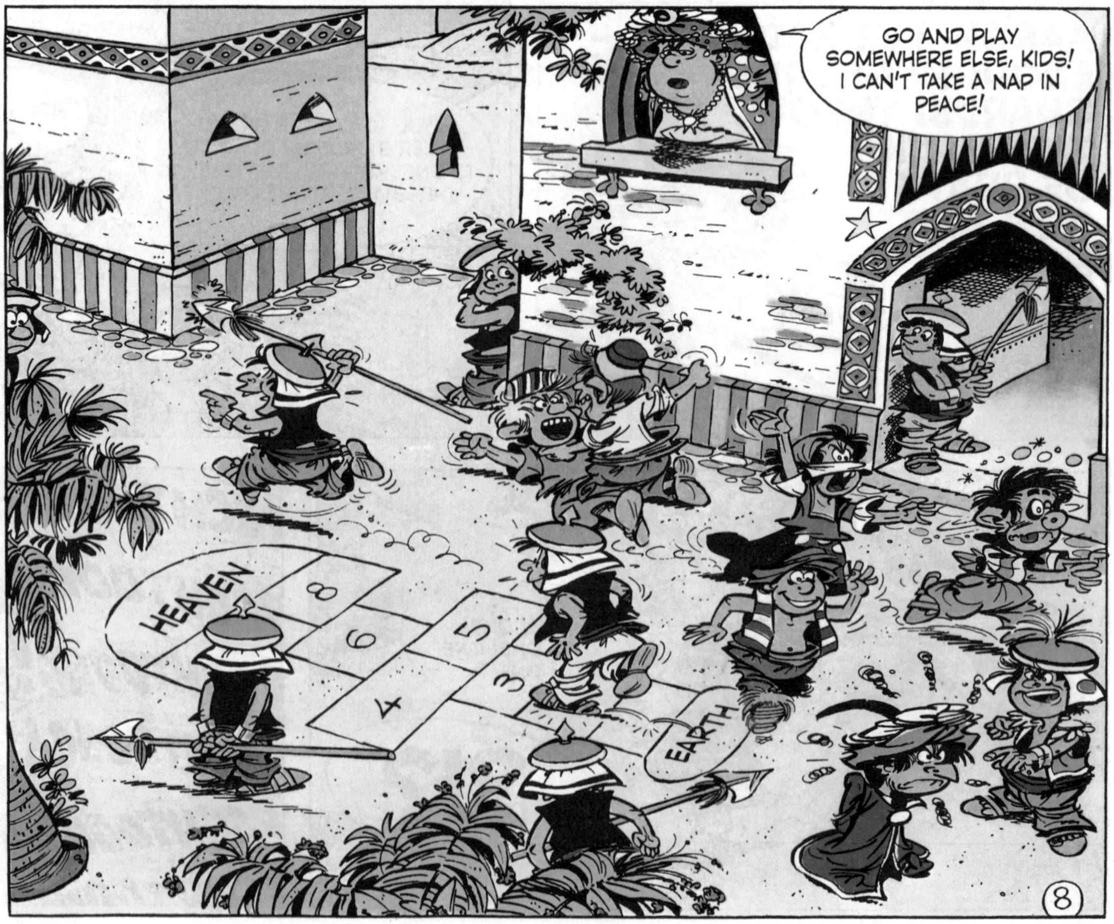
GO AND PLAY SOMEWHERE ELSE, KIDS! I CAN'T TAKE A NAP IN PEACE!
HEAVEN
EARTH

THE END

TEXT: GOSCINNY
ART: TABARY — 73

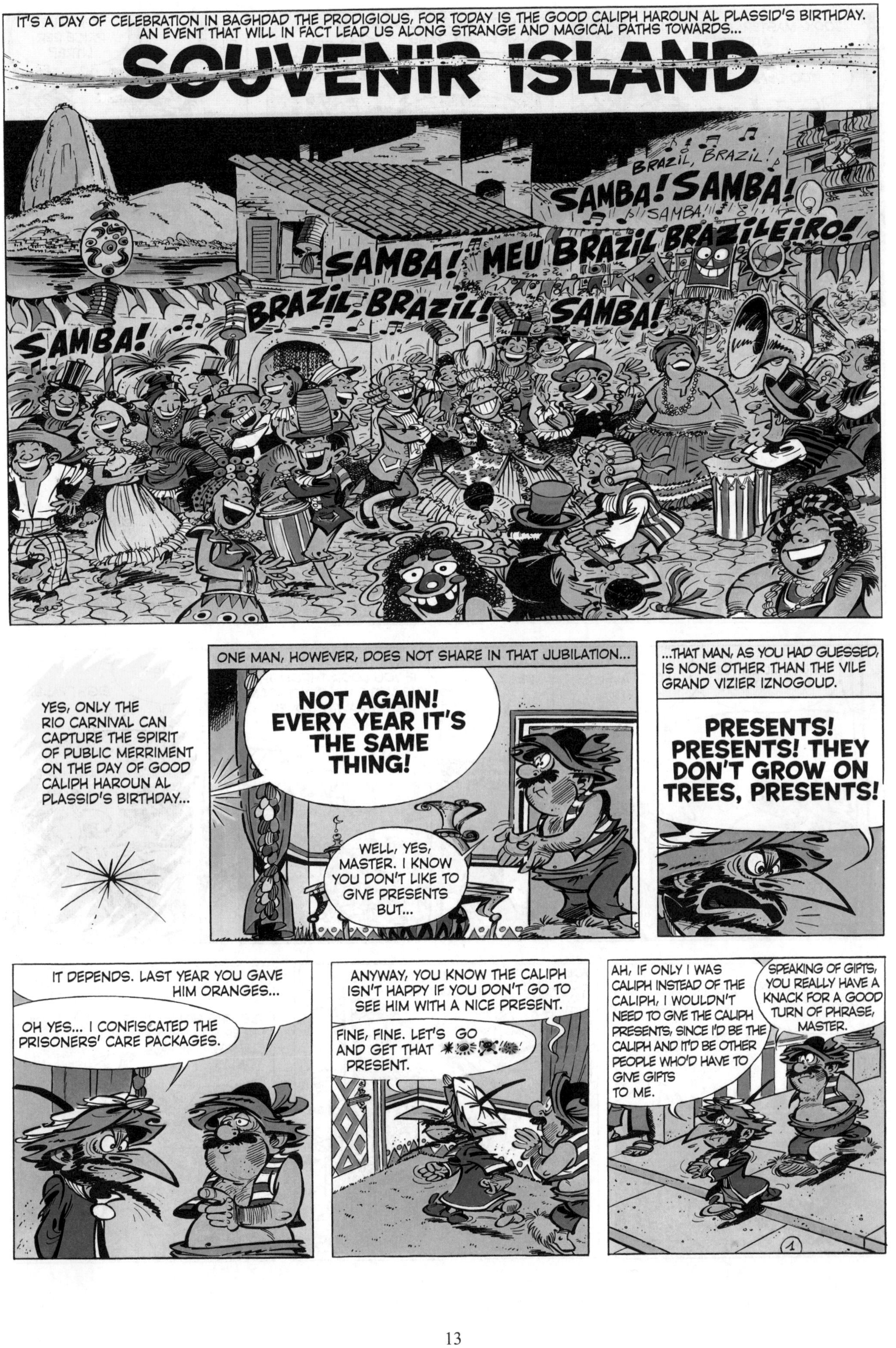

IT'S A DAY OF CELEBRATION IN BAGHDAD THE PRODIGIOUS, FOR TODAY IS THE GOOD CALIPH HAROUN AL PLASSID'S BIRTHDAY. AN EVENT THAT WILL IN FACT LEAD US ALONG STRANGE AND MAGICAL PATHS TOWARDS...
SOUVENIR ISLAND
BRAZIL, BRAZIL!
SAMBA! SAMBA!
SAMBA!
SAMBA! MEU BRAZIL BRAZILEIRO!
SAMBA!
BRAZIL, BRAZIL!
SAMBA!
YES, ONLY THE RIO CARNIVAL CAN CAPTURE THE SPIRIT OF PUBLIC MERRIMENT ON THE DAY OF GOOD CALIPH HAROUN AL PLASSID'S BIRTHDAY...
ONE MAN, HOWEVER, DOES NOT SHARE IN THAT JUBILATION...
NOT AGAIN! EVERY YEAR IT'S THE SAME THING!
WELL, YES, MASTER. I KNOW YOU DON'T LIKE TO GIVE PRESENTS BUT...
...THAT MAN, AS YOU HAD GUESSED, IS NONE OTHER THAN THE VILE GRAND VIZIER IZNOGOUD.
PRESENTS! PRESENTS! THEY DON'T GROW ON TREES, PRESENTS!
IT DEPENDS. LAST YEAR YOU GAVE HIM ORANGES...
OH YES... I CONFISCATED THE PRISONERS' CARE PACKAGES.
ANYWAY, YOU KNOW THE CALIPH ISN'T HAPPY IF YOU DON'T GO TO SEE HIM WITH A NICE PRESENT.
FINE, FINE. LET'S GO AND GET THAT PRESENT.
AH, IF ONLY I WAS CALIPH INSTEAD OF THE CALIPH, I WOULDN'T NEED TO GIVE THE CALIPH PRESENTS, SINCE I'D BE THE CALIPH AND IT'D BE OTHER PEOPLE WHO'D HAVE TO GIVE GIFTS TO ME.
SPEAKING OF GIFTS, YOU REALLY HAVE A KNACK FOR A GOOD TURN OF PHRASE, MASTER.

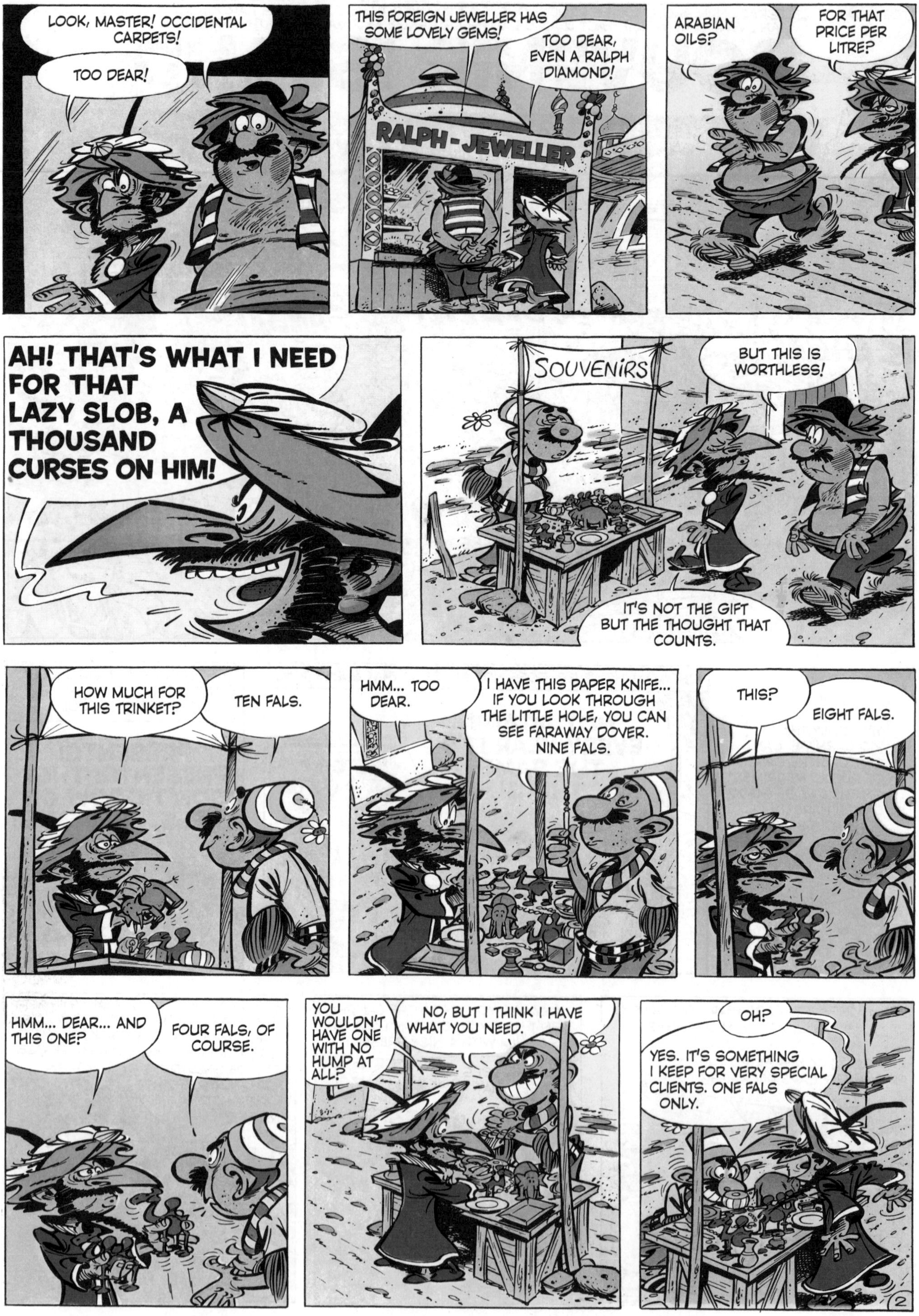
LOOK, MASTER! OCCIDENTAL CARPETS!
TOO DEAR!
THIS FOREIGN JEWELLER HAS SOME LOVELY GEMS!
TOO DEAR, EVEN A RALPH DIAMOND!
RALPH - JEWELLER
ARABIAN OILS?
FOR THAT PRICE PER LITRE?
AH! THAT'S WHAT I NEED FOR THAT LAZY SLOB, A THOUSAND CURSES ON HIM!
SOUVENIRS
BUT THIS IS WORTHLESS!
IT'S NOT THE GIFT BUT THE THOUGHT THAT COUNTS.
HOW MUCH FOR THIS TRINKET?
TEN FALS.
HMM... TOO DEAR.
I HAVE THIS PAPER KNIFE... IF YOU LOOK THROUGH THE LITTLE HOLE, YOU CAN SEE FARAWAY DOVER. NINE FALS.
THIS?
EIGHT FALS.
HMM... DEAR... AND THIS ONE?
FOUR FALS, OF COURSE.
YOU WOULDN'T HAVE ONE WITH NO HUMP AT ALL?
NO, BUT I THINK I HAVE WHAT YOU NEED.
OH?
YES. IT'S SOMETHING I KEEP FOR VERY SPECIAL CLIENTS. ONE FALS ONLY.
2

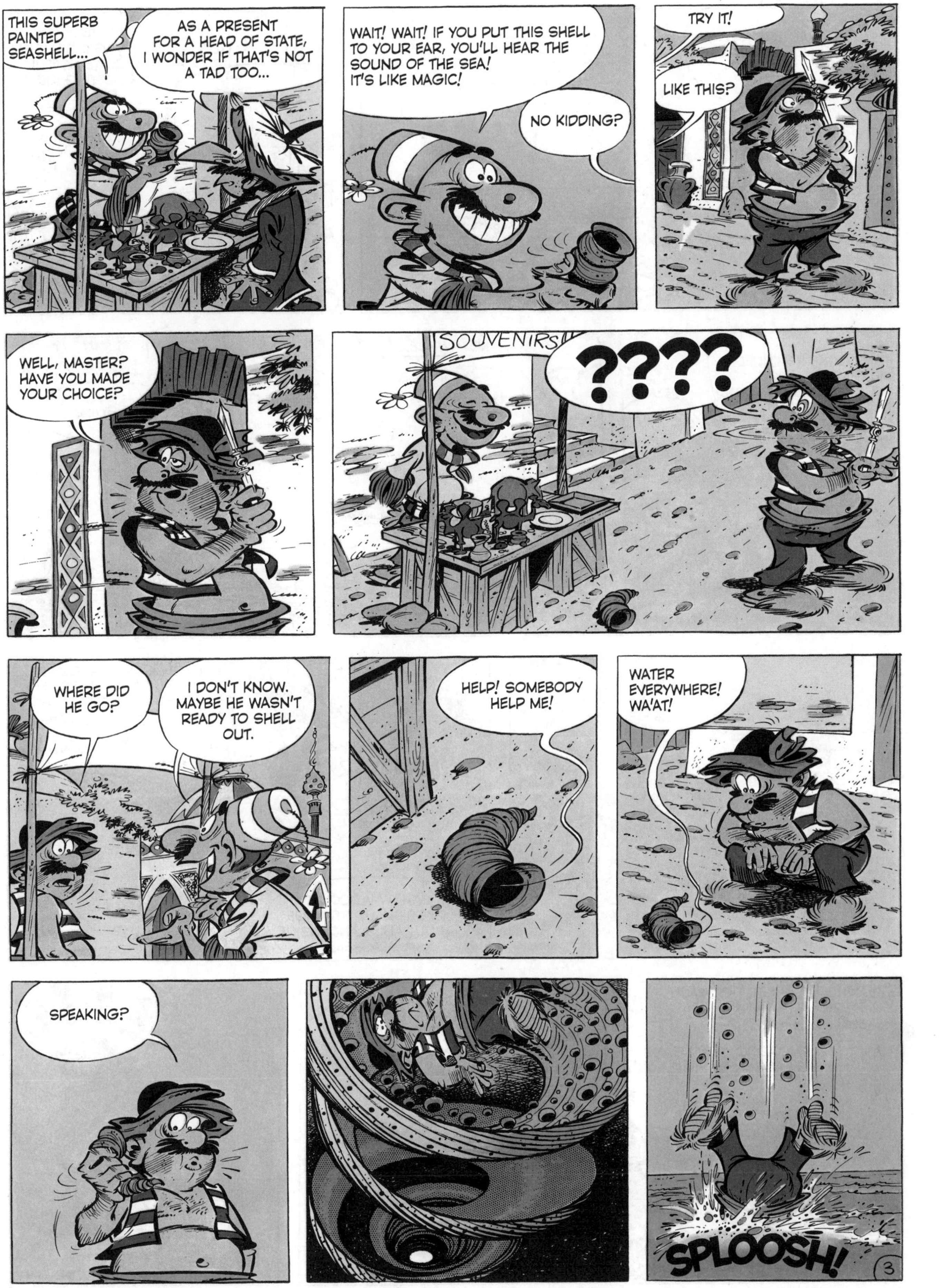
THIS SUPERB PAINTED SEASHELL...
AS A PRESENT FOR A HEAD OF STATE, I WONDER IF THAT'S NOT A TAD TOO...
WAIT! WAIT! IF YOU PUT THIS SHELL TO YOUR EAR, YOU'LL HEAR THE SOUND OF THE SEA! IT'S LIKE MAGIC!
NO KIDDING?
TRY IT!
LIKE THIS?
WELL, MASTER? HAVE YOU MADE YOUR CHOICE?
SOUVENIRS
????
WHERE DID HE GO?
I DON'T KNOW. MAYBE HE WASN'T READY TO SHELL OUT.
HELP! SOMEBODY HELP ME!
WATER EVERYWHERE! WA'AT!
SPEAKING?
SPLOOSH!
3

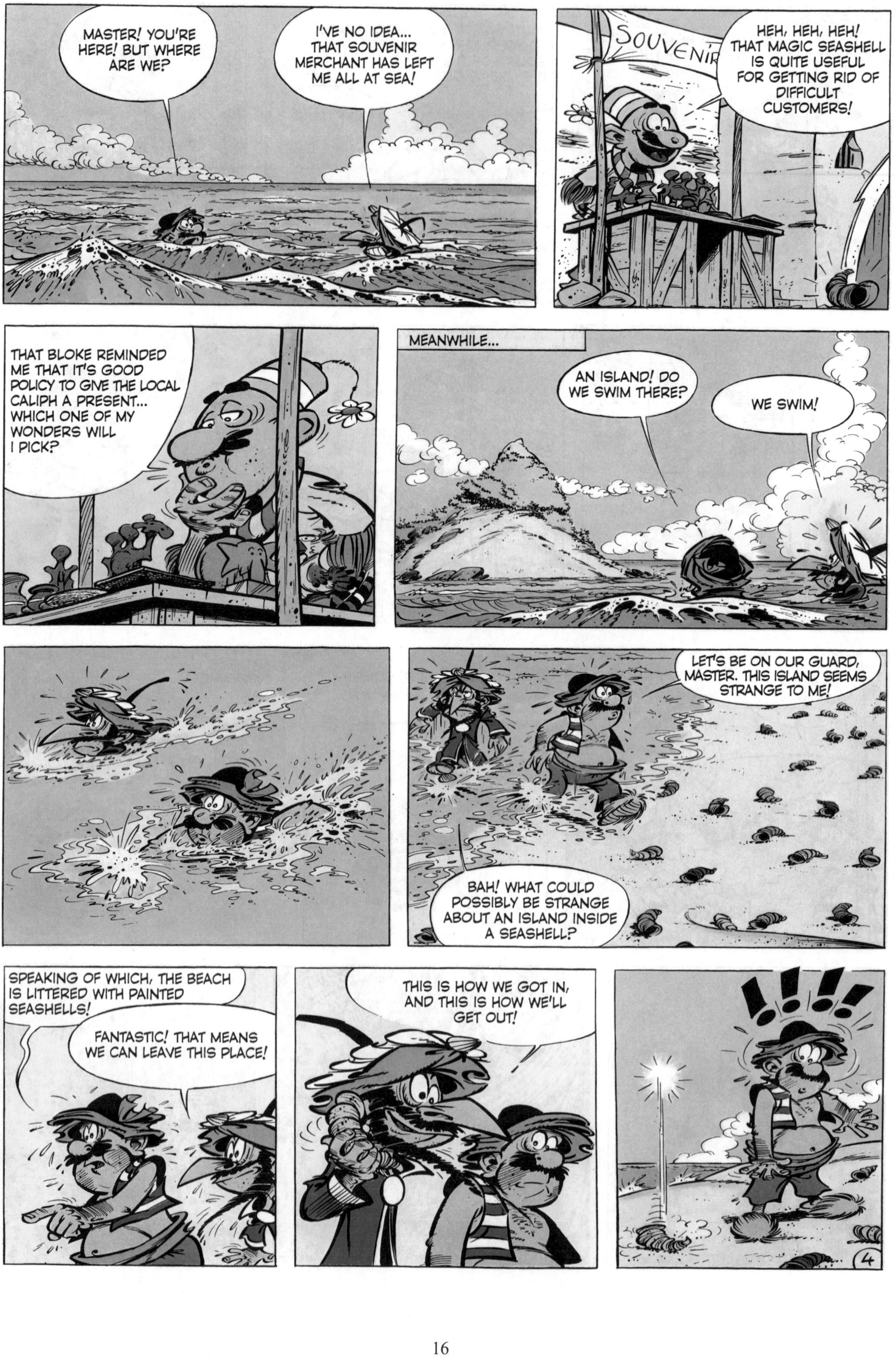
MASTER! YOU'RE HERE! BUT WHERE ARE WE?
I'VE NO IDEA... THAT SOUVENIR MERCHANT HAS LEFT ME ALL AT SEA!
SOUVENIR
HEH, HEH, HEH! THAT MAGIC SEASHELL IS QUITE USEFUL FOR GETTING RID OF DIFFICULT CUSTOMERS!
THAT BLOKE REMINDED ME THAT IT'S GOOD POLICY TO GIVE THE LOCAL CALIPH A PRESENT... WHICH ONE OF MY WONDERS WILL I PICK?
MEANWHILE...
AN ISLAND! DO WE SWIM THERE?
WE SWIM!
LET'S BE ON OUR GUARD, MASTER. THIS ISLAND SEEMS STRANGE TO ME!
BAH! WHAT COULD POSSIBLY BE STRANGE ABOUT AN ISLAND INSIDE A SEASHELL?
SPEAKING OF WHICH, THE BEACH IS LITTERED WITH PAINTED SEASHELLS!
FANTASTIC! THAT MEANS WE CAN LEAVE THIS PLACE!
THIS IS HOW WE GOT IN, AND THIS IS HOW WE'LL GET OUT!
!!!!
4

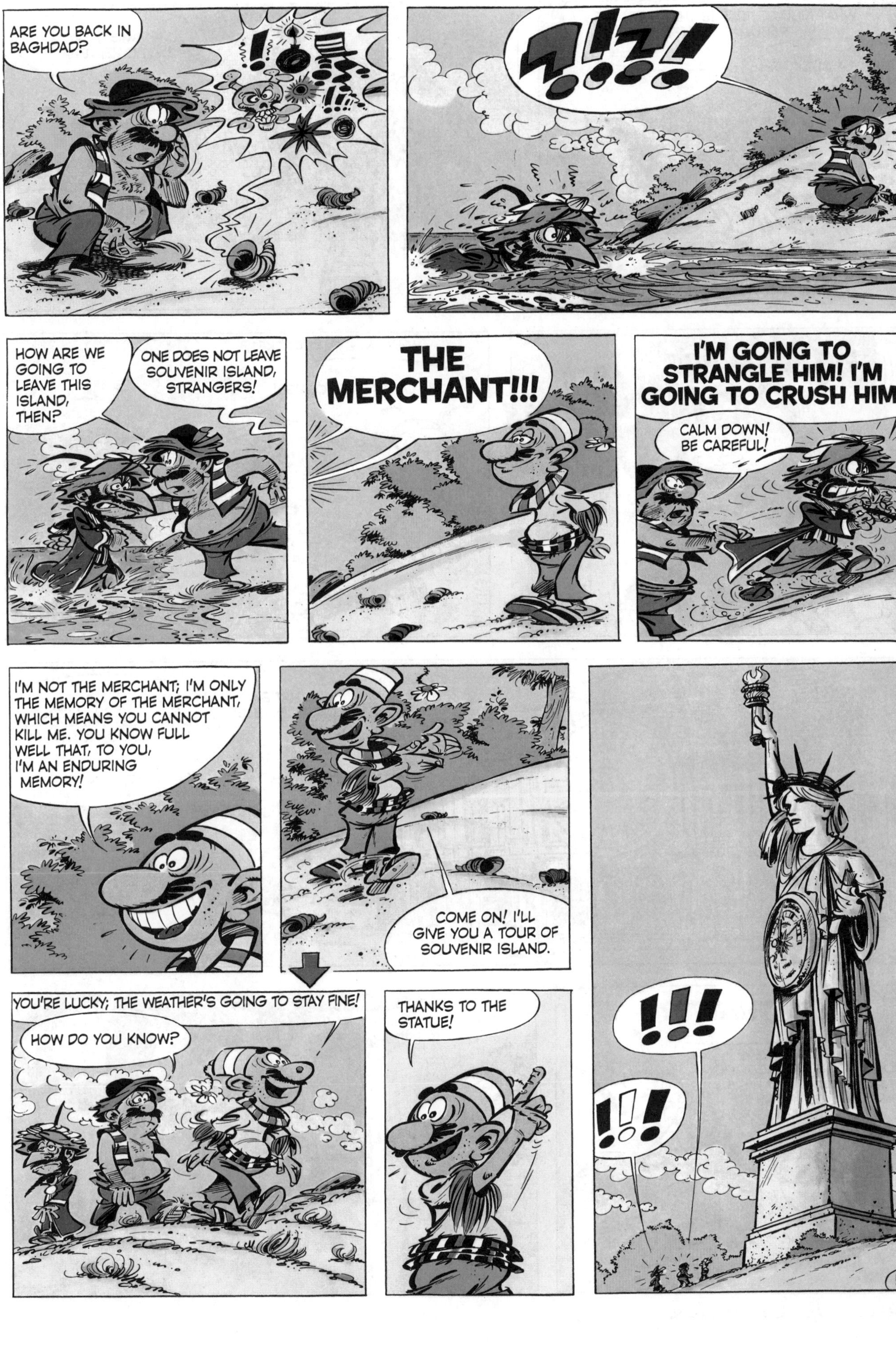

ARE YOU BACK IN BAGHDAD?
!!!
?!?!
HOW ARE WE GOING TO LEAVE THIS ISLAND, THEN?
ONE DOES NOT LEAVE SOUVENIR ISLAND, STRANGERS!
THE MERCHANT!!!
I'M GOING TO STRANGLE HIM! I'M GOING TO CRUSH HIM!
CALM DOWN! BE CAREFUL!
I'M NOT THE MERCHANT; I'M ONLY THE MEMORY OF THE MERCHANT, WHICH MEANS YOU CANNOT KILL ME. YOU KNOW FULL WELL THAT, TO YOU, I'M AN ENDURING MEMORY!
COME ON! I'LL GIVE YOU A TOUR OF SOUVENIR ISLAND.
YOU'RE LUCKY; THE WEATHER'S GOING TO STAY FINE!
HOW DO YOU KNOW?
THANKS TO THE STATUE!
!!!
!?!
5

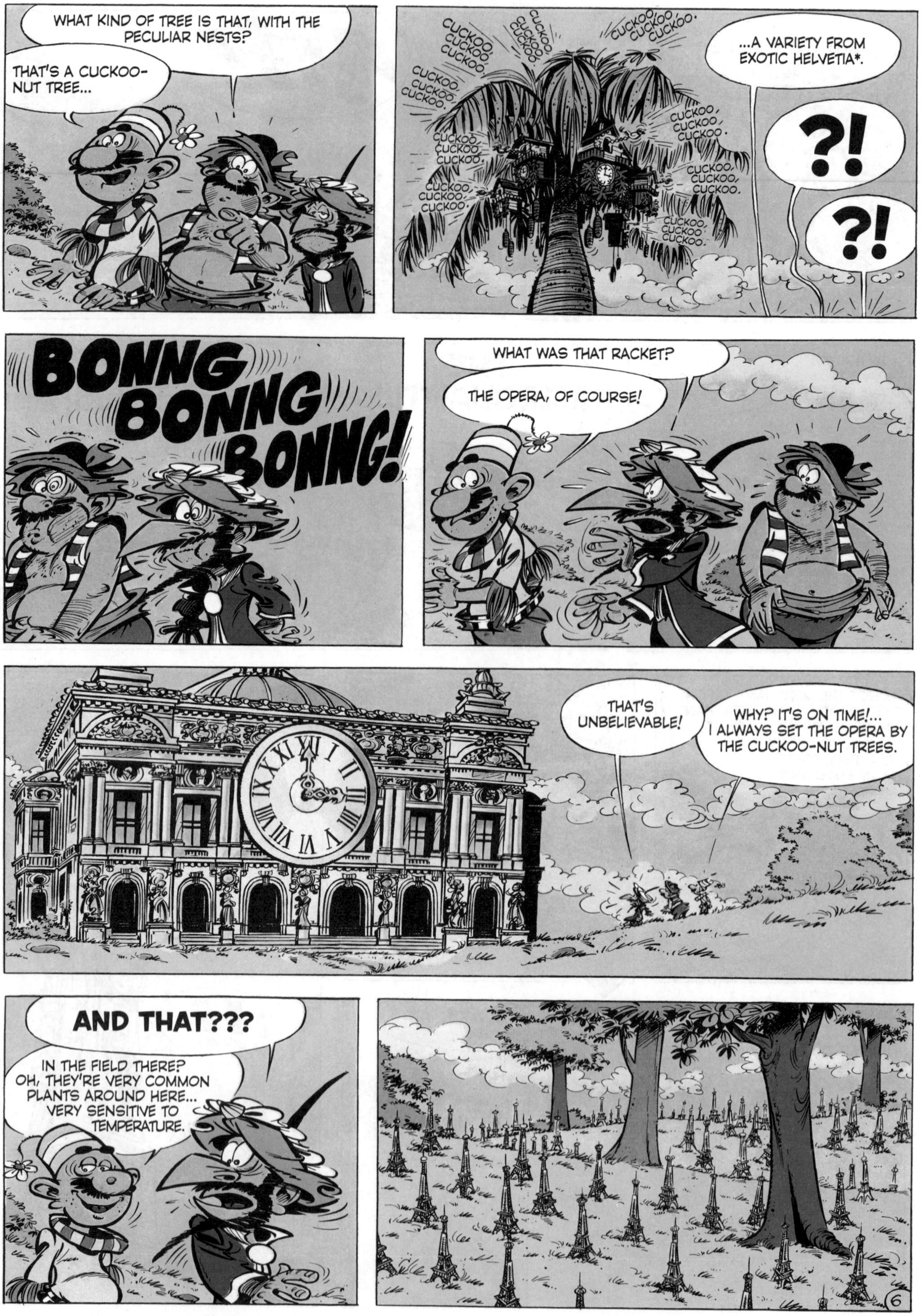
WHAT KIND OF TREE IS THAT, WITH THE PECULIAR NESTS?
THAT'S A CUCKOO-NUT TREE...
CUCKOO, CUCKOO, CUCKOO.
...A VARIETY FROM EXOTIC HELVETIA*.
?!
?!
BONNG BONNG BONNG!
WHAT WAS THAT RACKET?
THE OPERA, OF COURSE!
THAT'S UNBELIEVABLE!
WHY? IT'S ON TIME!... I ALWAYS SET THE OPERA BY THE CUCKOO-NUT TREES.
AND THAT???
IN THE FIELD THERE? OH, THEY'RE VERY COMMON PLANTS AROUND HERE... VERY SENSITIVE TO TEMPERATURE.
6

*THE LATIN NAME FOR SWITZERLAND

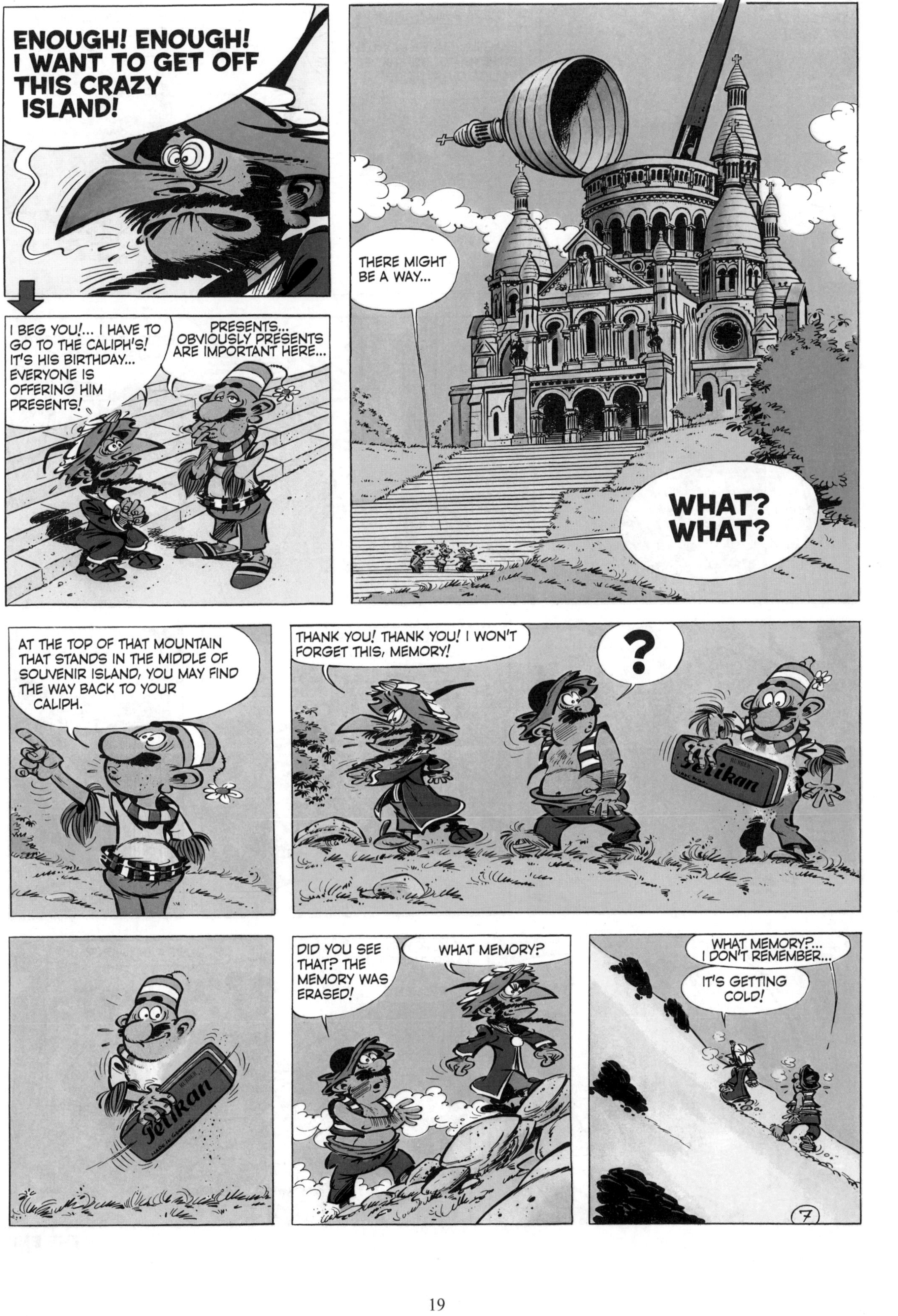
ENOUGH! ENOUGH! I WANT TO GET OFF THIS CRAZY ISLAND!
I BEG YOU!... I HAVE TO GO TO THE CALIPH'S! IT'S HIS BIRTHDAY... EVERYONE IS OFFERING HIM PRESENTS!
PRESENTS... OBVIOUSLY PRESENTS ARE IMPORTANT HERE...
THERE MIGHT BE A WAY...
WHAT? WHAT?
AT THE TOP OF THAT MOUNTAIN THAT STANDS IN THE MIDDLE OF SOUVENIR ISLAND, YOU MAY FIND THE WAY BACK TO YOUR CALIPH.
THANK YOU! THANK YOU! I WON'T FORGET THIS, MEMORY!
?
Pelikan
Pelikan
DID YOU SEE THAT? THE MEMORY WAS ERASED!
WHAT MEMORY?
WHAT MEMORY?... I DON'T REMEMBER...
IT'S GETTING COLD!
7

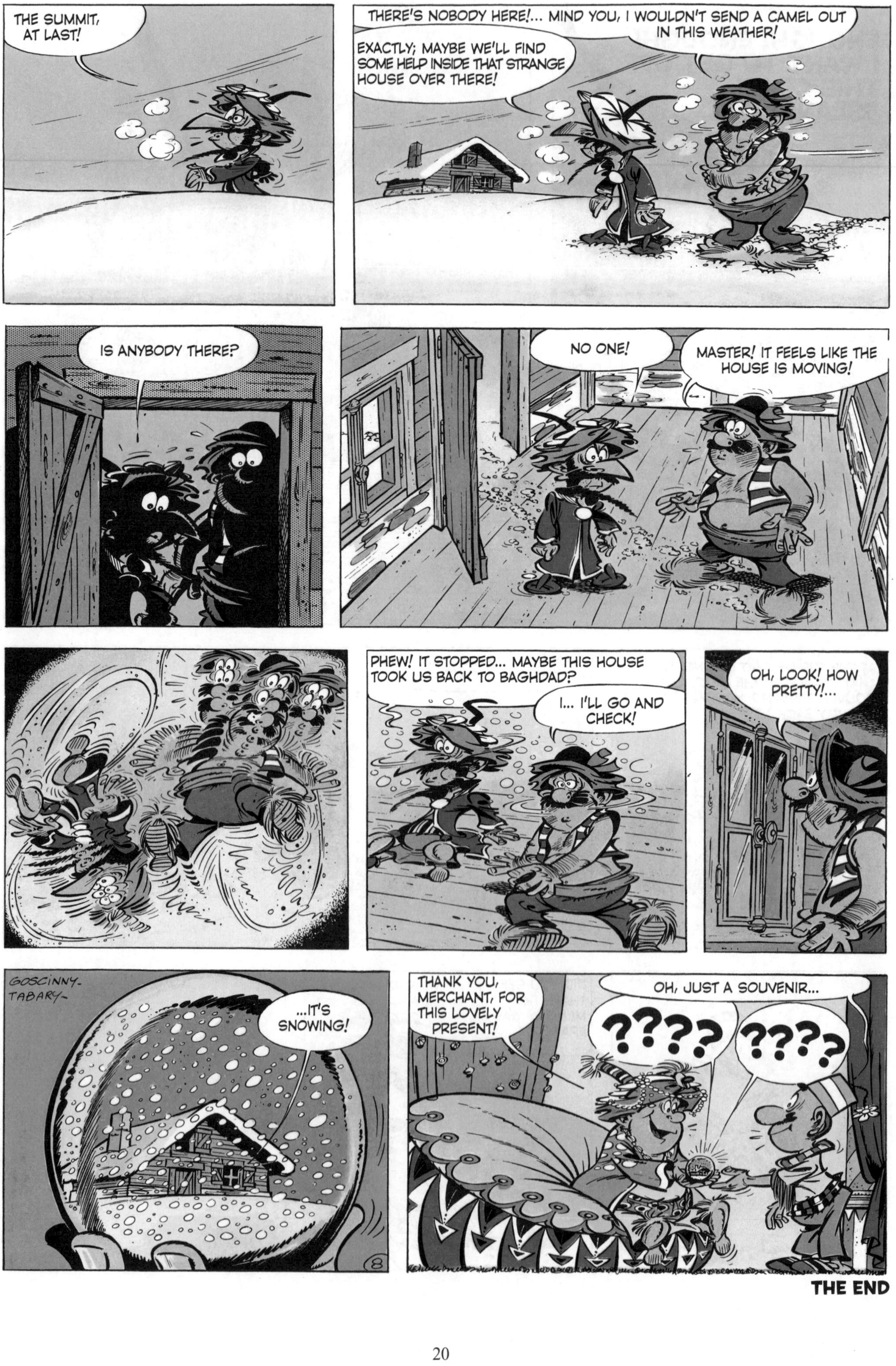
THE SUMMIT, AT LAST!
THERE'S NOBODY HERE!... MIND YOU, I WOULDN'T SEND A CAMEL OUT IN THIS WEATHER!
EXACTLY; MAYBE WE'LL FIND SOME HELP INSIDE THAT STRANGE HOUSE OVER THERE!
IS ANYBODY THERE?
NO ONE!
MASTER! IT FEELS LIKE THE HOUSE IS MOVING!
PHEW! IT STOPPED... MAYBE THIS HOUSE TOOK US BACK TO BAGHDAD?
I... I'LL GO AND CHECK!
OH, LOOK! HOW PRETTY!...
GOSCINNY-TABARY-
...IT'S SNOWING!
8
THANK YOU, MERCHANT, FOR THIS LOVELY PRESENT!
OH, JUST A SOUVENIR...
????
????

THE END

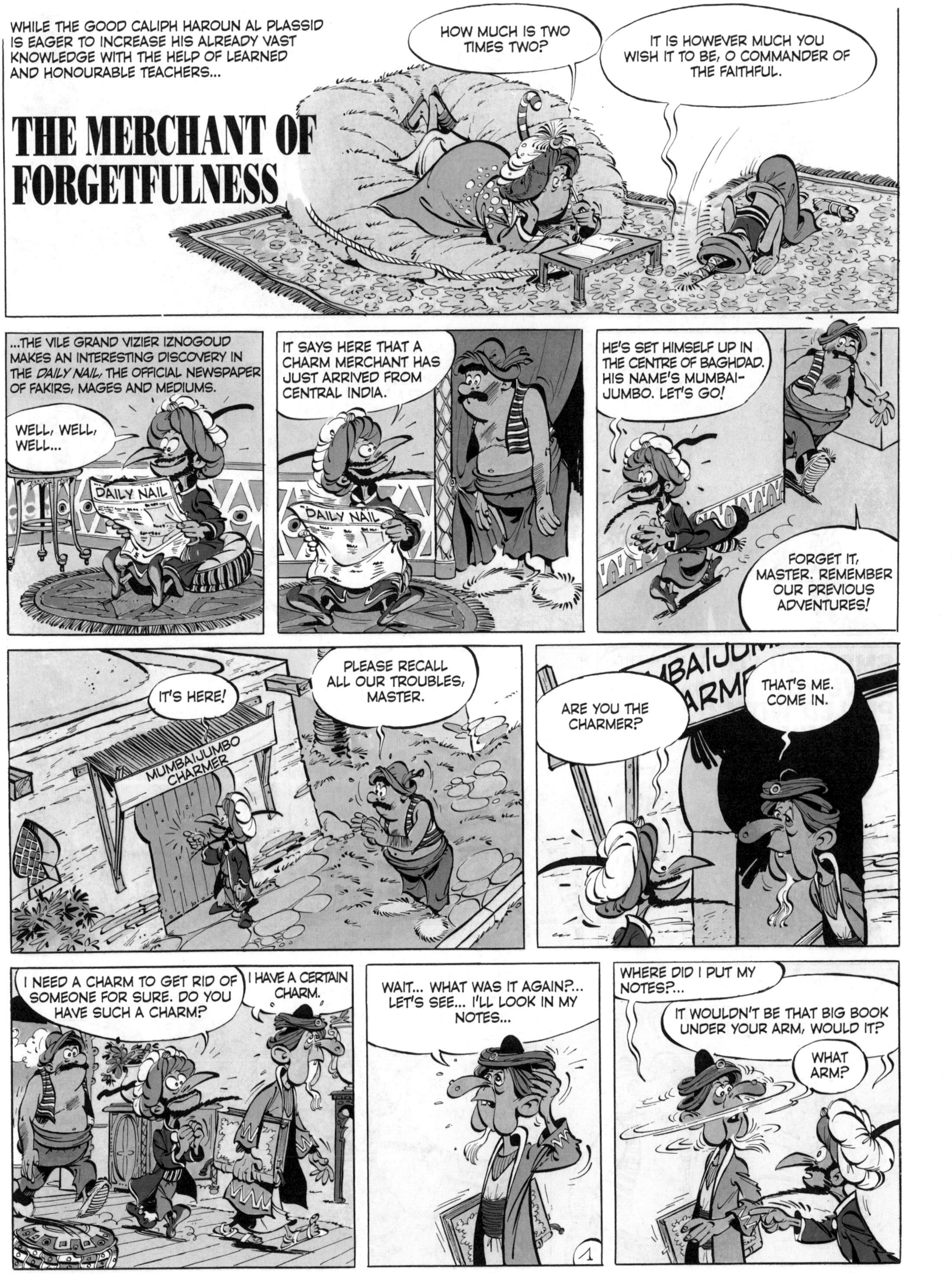
WHILE THE GOOD CALIPH HAROUN AL PLASSID IS EAGER TO INCREASE HIS ALREADY VAST KNOWLEDGE WITH THE HELP OF LEARNED AND HONOURABLE TEACHERS...
THE MERCHANT OF FORGETFULNESS
HOW MUCH IS TWO TIMES TWO?
IT IS HOWEVER MUCH YOU WISH IT TO BE, O COMMANDER OF THE FAITHFUL.
...THE VILE GRAND VIZIER IZNOGOUD MAKES AN INTERESTING DISCOVERY IN THE DAILY NAIL, THE OFFICIAL NEWSPAPER OF FAKIRS, MAGES AND MEDIUMS.
WELL, WELL, WELL...
DAILY NAIL
IT SAYS HERE THAT A CHARM MERCHANT HAS JUST ARRIVED FROM CENTRAL INDIA.
DAILY NAIL
HE'S SET HIMSELF UP IN THE CENTRE OF BAGHDAD. HIS NAME'S MUMBAI-JUMBO. LET'S GO!
FORGET IT, MASTER. REMEMBER OUR PREVIOUS ADVENTURES!
IT'S HERE!
PLEASE RECALL ALL OUR TROUBLES, MASTER.
MUMBAIJUMBO CHARMER
ARE YOU THE CHARMER?
THAT'S ME. COME IN.
I NEED A CHARM TO GET RID OF SOMEONE FOR SURE. DO YOU HAVE SUCH A CHARM?
I HAVE A CERTAIN CHARM.
WAIT... WHAT WAS IT AGAIN?... LET'S SEE... I'LL LOOK IN MY NOTES...
WHERE DID I PUT MY NOTES?...
IT WOULDN'T BE THAT BIG BOOK UNDER YOUR ARM, WOULD IT?
WHAT ARM?
1

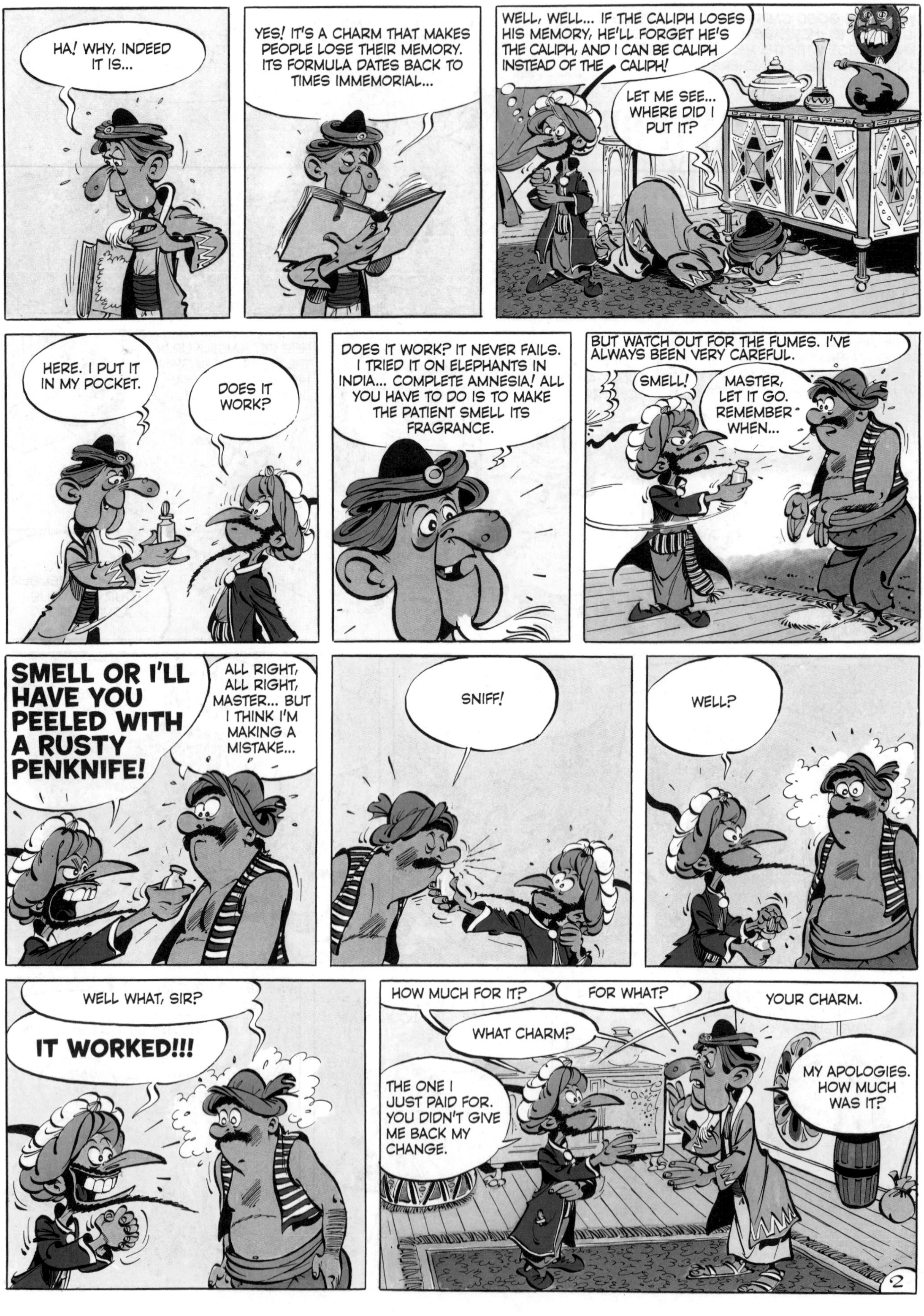
HA! WHY, INDEED IT IS...
YES! IT'S A CHARM THAT MAKES PEOPLE LOSE THEIR MEMORY. ITS FORMULA DATES BACK TO TIMES IMMEMORIAL...
WELL, WELL... IF THE CALIPH LOSES HIS MEMORY, HE'LL FORGET HE'S THE CALIPH, AND I CAN BE CALIPH INSTEAD OF THE CALIPH!
LET ME SEE... WHERE DID I PUT IT?
HERE. I PUT IT IN MY POCKET.
DOES IT WORK?
DOES IT WORK? IT NEVER FAILS. I TRIED IT ON ELEPHANTS IN INDIA... COMPLETE AMNESIA! ALL YOU HAVE TO DO IS TO MAKE THE PATIENT SMELL ITS FRAGRANCE.
BUT WATCH OUT FOR THE FUMES. I'VE ALWAYS BEEN VERY CAREFUL.
SMELL!
MASTER, LET IT GO. REMEMBER WHEN...
SMELL OR I'LL HAVE YOU PEELED WITH A RUSTY PENKNIFE!
ALL RIGHT, ALL RIGHT, MASTER... BUT I THINK I'M MAKING A MISTAKE...
SNIFF!
WELL?
WELL WHAT, SIR?
IT WORKED!!!
HOW MUCH FOR IT?
FOR WHAT?
YOUR CHARM.
WHAT CHARM?
THE ONE I JUST PAID FOR. YOU DIDN'T GIVE ME BACK MY CHANGE.
MY APOLOGIES. HOW MUCH WAS IT?
2

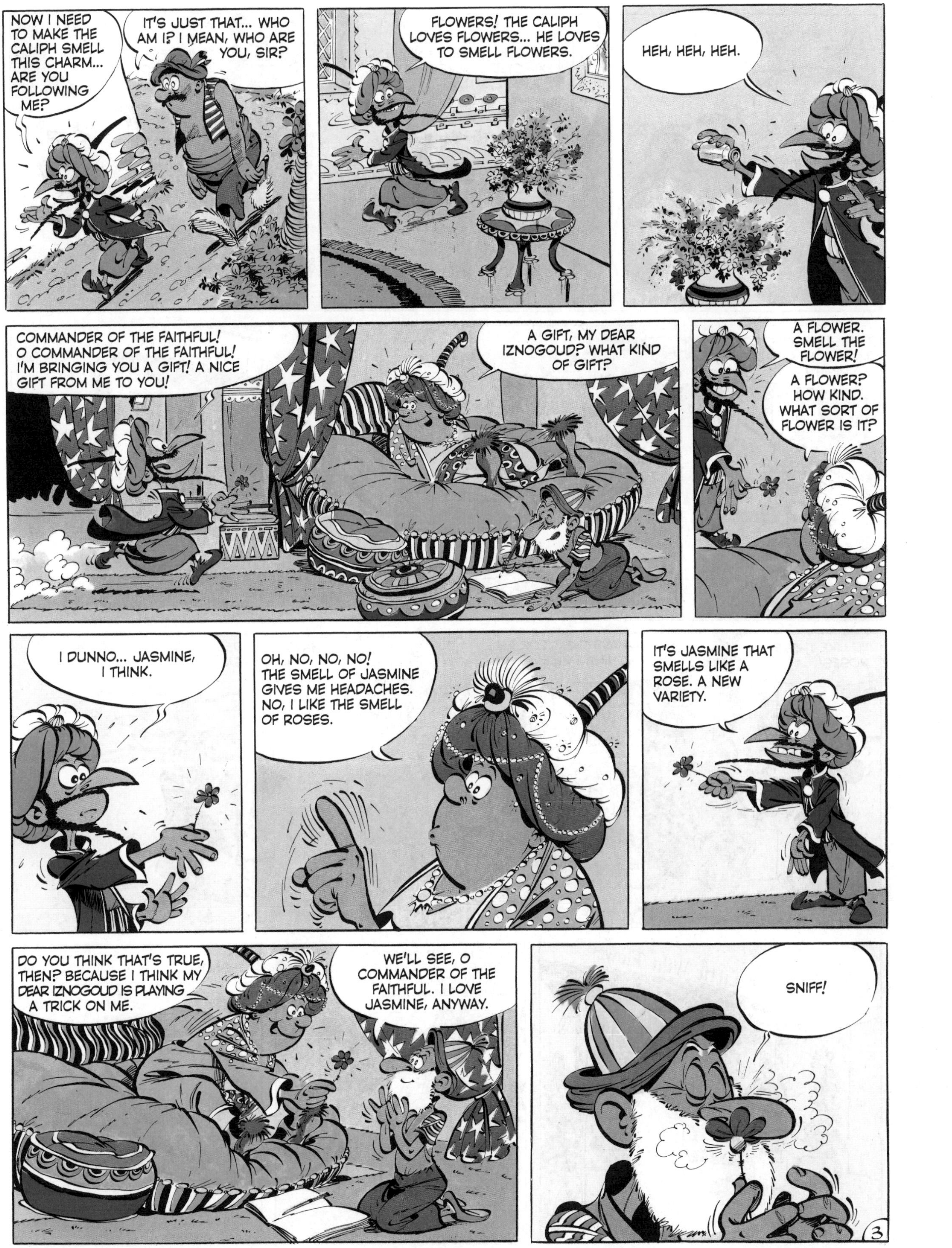
NOW I NEED TO MAKE THE CALIPH SMELL THIS CHARM... ARE YOU FOLLOWING ME?
IT'S JUST THAT... WHO AM I? I MEAN, WHO ARE YOU, SIR?
FLOWERS! THE CALIPH LOVES FLOWERS... HE LOVES TO SMELL FLOWERS.
HEH, HEH, HEH.
COMMANDER OF THE FAITHFUL! O COMMANDER OF THE FAITHFUL! I'M BRINGING YOU A GIFT! A NICE GIFT FROM ME TO YOU!
A GIFT, MY DEAR IZNOGOUD? WHAT KIND OF GIFT?
A FLOWER. SMELL THE FLOWER!
A FLOWER? HOW KIND. WHAT SORT OF FLOWER IS IT?
I DUNNO... JASMINE, I THINK.
OH, NO, NO, NO! THE SMELL OF JASMINE GIVES ME HEADACHES. NO, I LIKE THE SMELL OF ROSES.
IT'S JASMINE THAT SMELLS LIKE A ROSE. A NEW VARIETY.
DO YOU THINK THAT'S TRUE, THEN? BECAUSE I THINK MY DEAR IZNOGOUD IS PLAYING A TRICK ON ME.
WE'LL SEE, O COMMANDER OF THE FAITHFUL. I LOVE JASMINE, ANYWAY.
SNIFF!
3

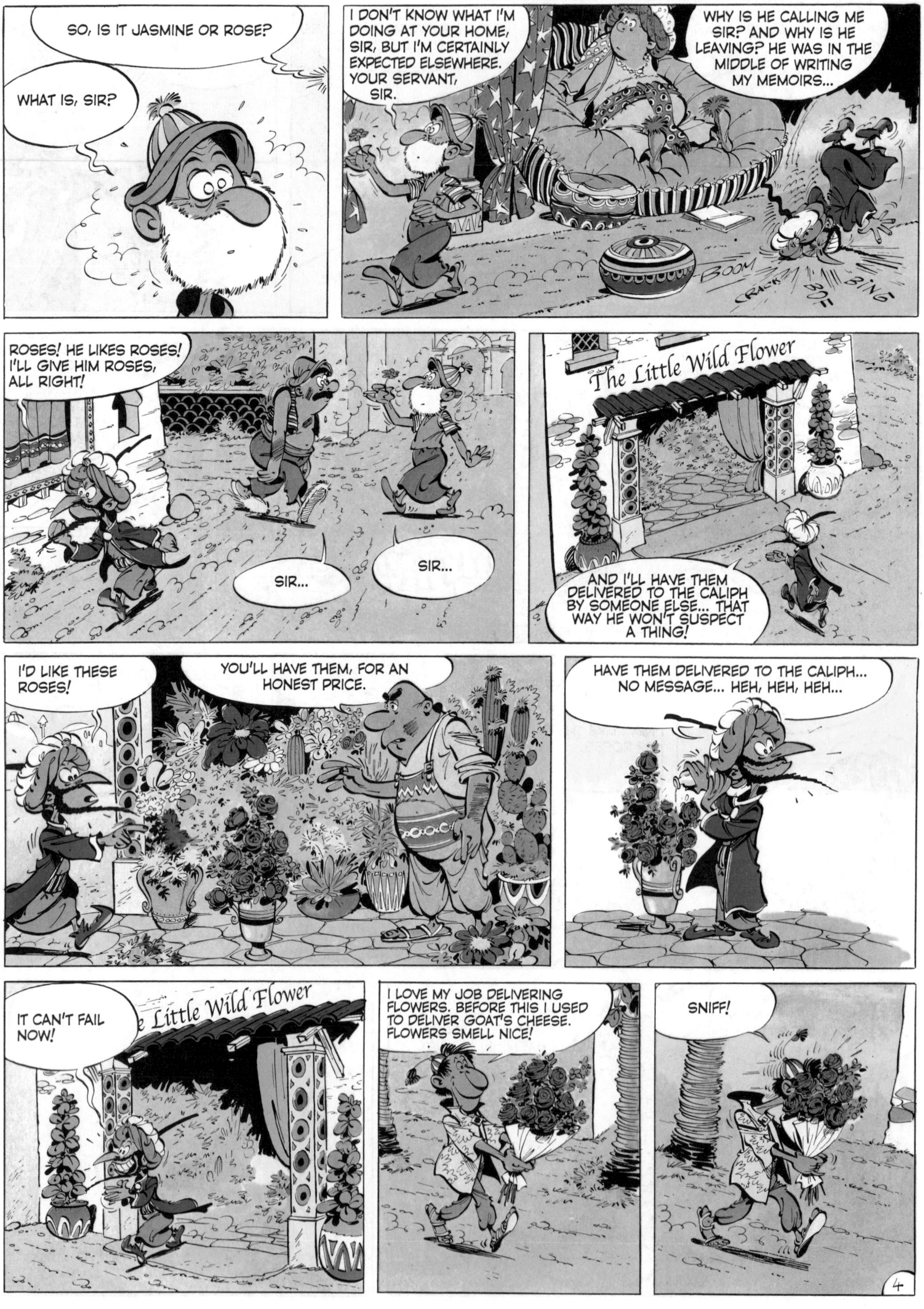
SO, IS IT JASMINE OR ROSE?
WHAT IS, SIR?
I DON'T KNOW WHAT I'M DOING AT YOUR HOME, SIR, BUT I'M CERTAINLY EXPECTED ELSEWHERE. YOUR SERVANT, SIR.
WHY IS HE CALLING ME SIR? AND WHY IS HE LEAVING? HE WAS IN THE MIDDLE OF WRITING MY MEMOIRS...
BOOM
CRACK
BOF
BING
ROSES! HE LIKES ROSES! I'LL GIVE HIM ROSES, ALL RIGHT!
SIR...
SIR...
The Little Wild Flower
AND I'LL HAVE THEM DELIVERED TO THE CALIPH BY SOMEONE ELSE... THAT WAY HE WON'T SUSPECT A THING!
I'D LIKE THESE ROSES!
YOU'LL HAVE THEM, FOR AN HONEST PRICE.
HAVE THEM DELIVERED TO THE CALIPH... NO MESSAGE... HEH, HEH, HEH...
IT CAN'T FAIL NOW!
e Little Wild Flower
I LOVE MY JOB DELIVERING FLOWERS. BEFORE THIS I USED TO DELIVER GOAT'S CHEESE. FLOWERS SMELL NICE!
SNIFF!
4

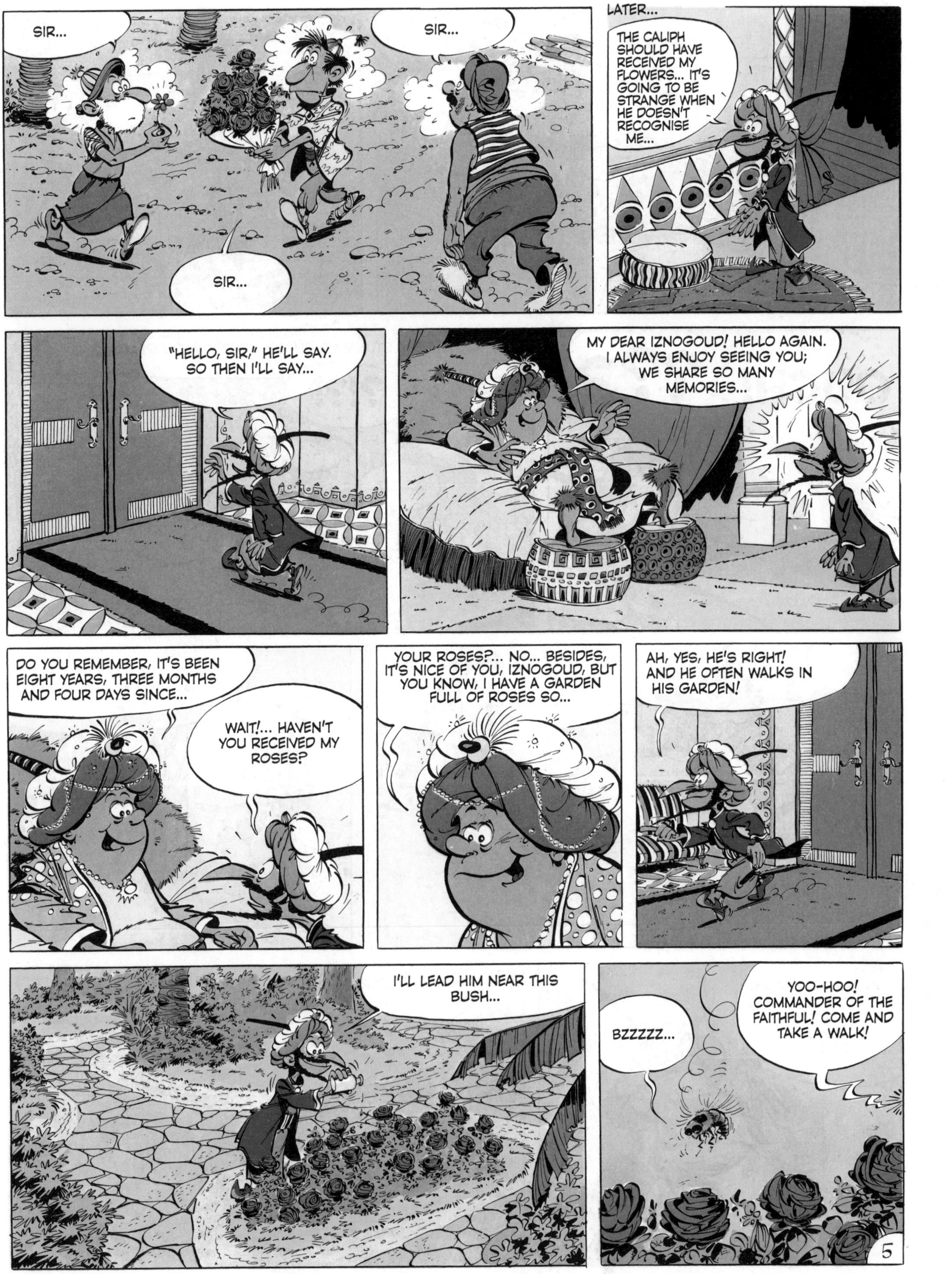
SIR...
SIR...
SIR...
LATER...
THE CALIPH SHOULD HAVE RECEIVED MY FLOWERS... IT'S GOING TO BE STRANGE WHEN HE DOESN'T RECOGNISE ME...
"HELLO, SIR," HE'LL SAY. SO THEN I'LL SAY...
MY DEAR IZNOGOUD! HELLO AGAIN. I ALWAYS ENJOY SEEING YOU; WE SHARE SO MANY MEMORIES...
DO YOU REMEMBER, IT'S BEEN EIGHT YEARS, THREE MONTHS AND FOUR DAYS SINCE...
WAIT!... HAVEN'T YOU RECEIVED MY ROSES?
YOUR ROSES?... NO... BESIDES, IT'S NICE OF YOU, IZNOGOUD, BUT YOU KNOW, I HAVE A GARDEN FULL OF ROSES SO...
AH, YES, HE'S RIGHT! AND HE OFTEN WALKS IN HIS GARDEN!
I'LL LEAD HIM NEAR THIS BUSH...
BZZZZZ...
YOO-HOO! COMMANDER OF THE FAITHFUL! COME AND TAKE A WALK!
5

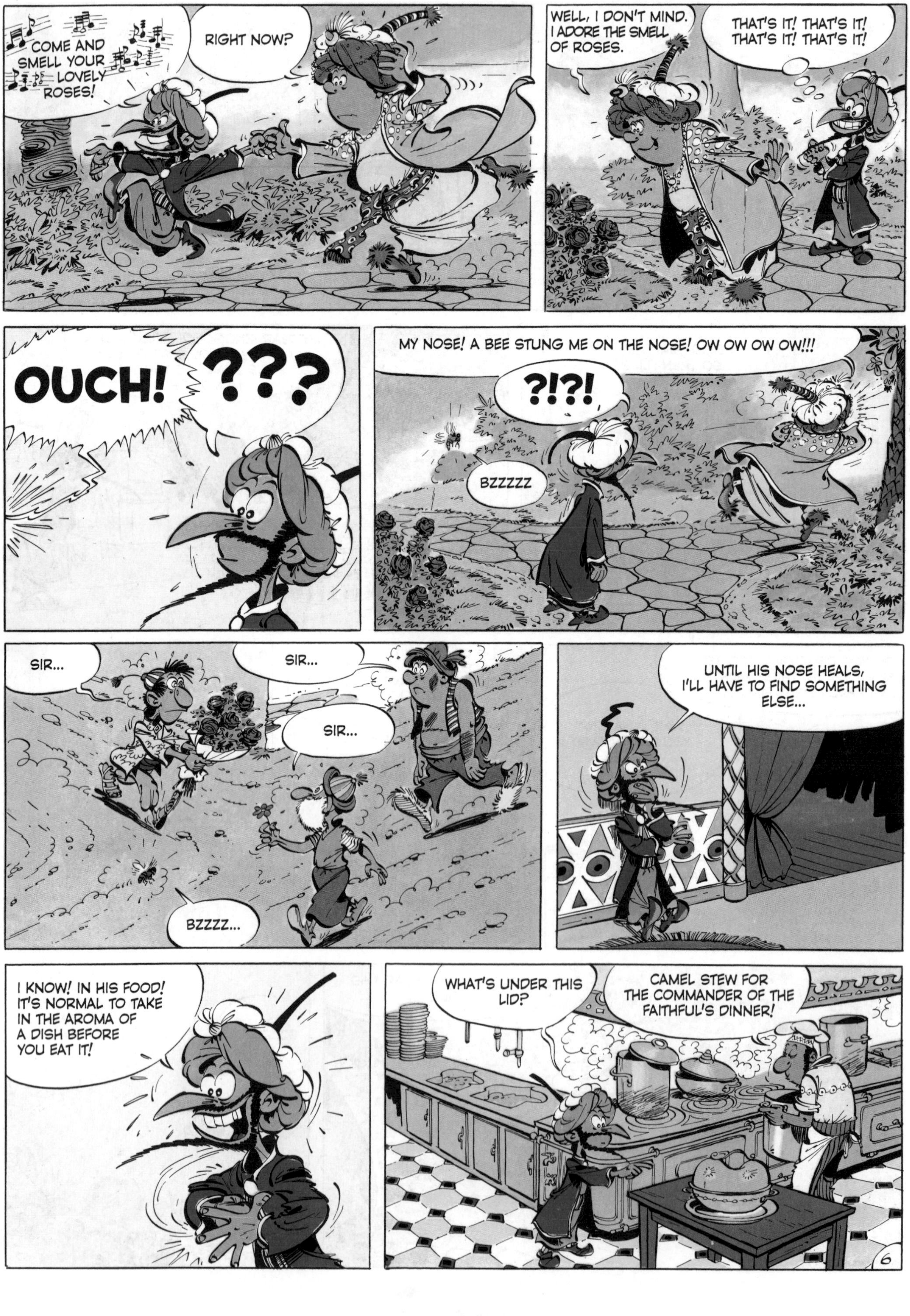
COME AND SMELL YOUR LOVELY ROSES!
RIGHT NOW?
WELL, I DON'T MIND. I ADORE THE SMELL OF ROSES.
THAT'S IT! THAT'S IT! THAT'S IT! THAT'S IT!
OUCH!
???
MY NOSE! A BEE STUNG ME ON THE NOSE! OW OW OW OW!!!
?!?!
BZZZZZ
SIR...
SIR...
SIR...
BZZZZ...
UNTIL HIS NOSE HEALS, I'LL HAVE TO FIND SOMETHING ELSE...
I KNOW! IN HIS FOOD! IT'S NORMAL TO TAKE IN THE AROMA OF A DISH BEFORE YOU EAT IT!
WHAT'S UNDER THIS LID?
CAMEL STEW FOR THE COMMANDER OF THE FAITHFUL'S DINNER!
6

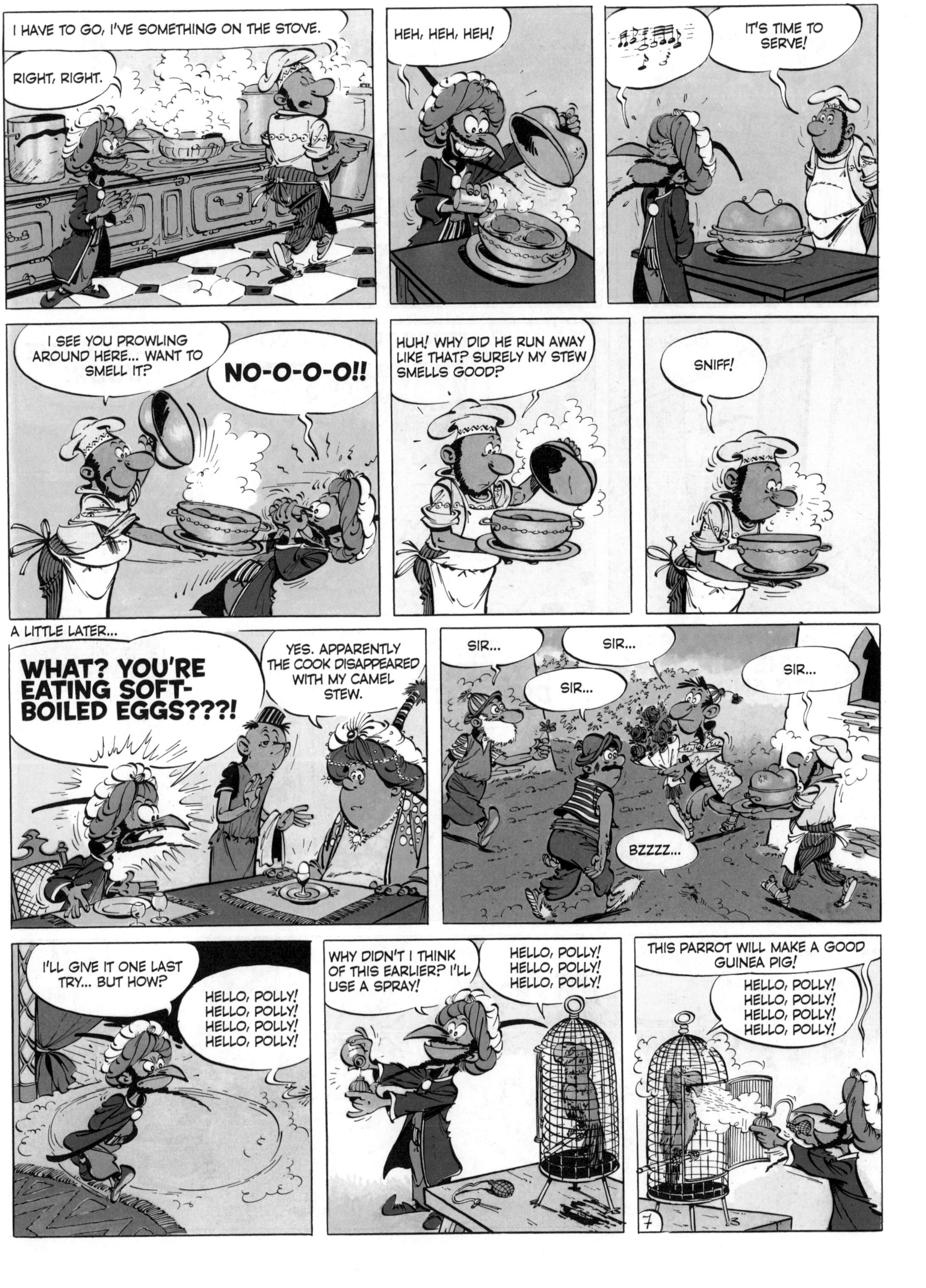
I HAVE TO GO, I'VE SOMETHING ON THE STOVE.
RIGHT, RIGHT.
HEH, HEH, HEH!
IT'S TIME TO SERVE!
I SEE YOU PROWLING AROUND HERE... WANT TO SMELL IT?
NO-O-O-O!!
HUH! WHY DID HE RUN AWAY LIKE THAT? SURELY MY STEW SMELLS GOOD?
SNIFF!
A LITTLE LATER...
WHAT? YOU'RE EATING SOFT-BOILED EGGS???!
YES. APPARENTLY THE COOK DISAPPEARED WITH MY CAMEL STEW.
SIR...
SIR...
SIR...
SIR...
BZZZZ...
I'LL GIVE IT ONE LAST TRY... BUT HOW?
HELLO, POLLY! HELLO, POLLY! HELLO, POLLY! HELLO, POLLY!
WHY DIDN'T I THINK OF THIS EARLIER? I'LL USE A SPRAY!
HELLO, POLLY! HELLO, POLLY! HELLO, POLLY!
THIS PARROT WILL MAKE A GOOD GUINEA PIG!
HELLO, POLLY! HELLO, POLLY! HELLO, POLLY! HELLO, POLLY!
7

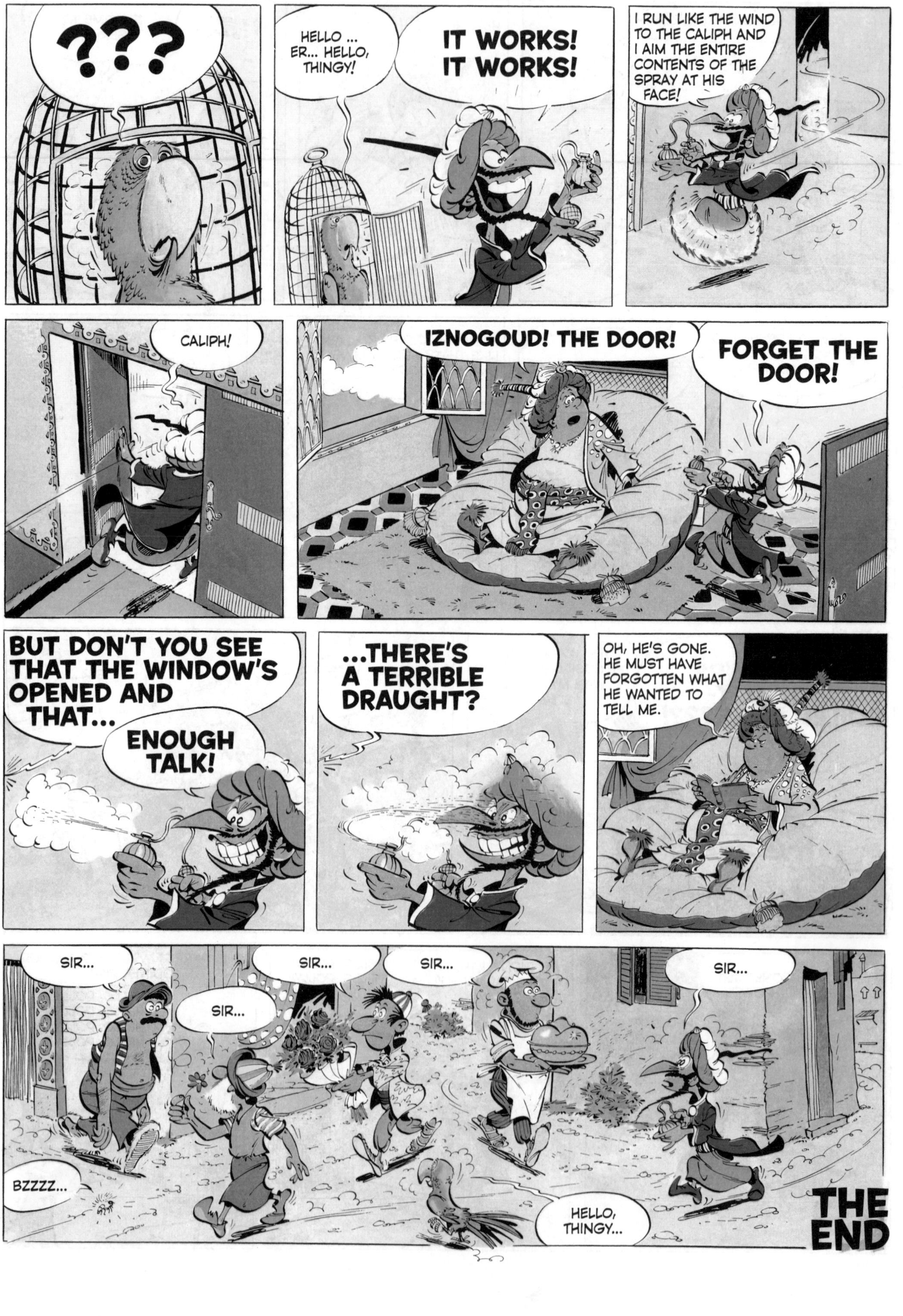
???
HELLO ... ER... HELLO, THINGY!
IT WORKS! IT WORKS!
I RUN LIKE THE WIND TO THE CALIPH AND I AIM THE ENTIRE CONTENTS OF THE SPRAY AT HIS FACE!
CALIPH!
IZNOGOUD! THE DOOR!
FORGET THE DOOR!
BUT DON'T YOU SEE THAT THE WINDOW'S OPENED AND THAT...
ENOUGH TALK!
...THERE'S A TERRIBLE DRAUGHT?
OH, HE'S GONE. HE MUST HAVE FORGOTTEN WHAT HE WANTED TO TELL ME.
SIR...
SIR...
SIR...
SIR...
SIR...
BZZZZ...
HELLO, THINGY...
THE END

The doggy flute

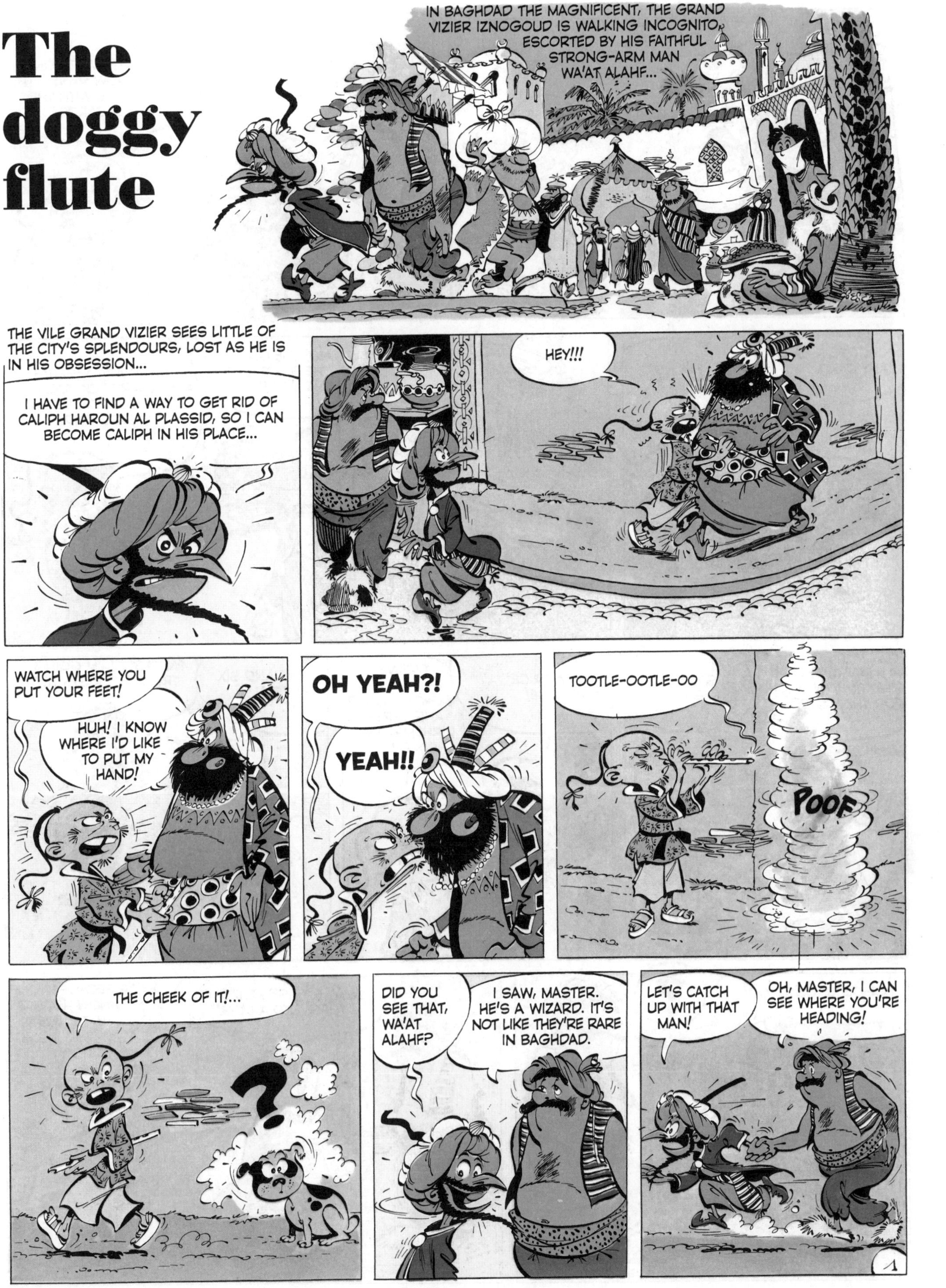
IN BAGHDAD THE MAGNIFICENT, THE GRAND VIZIER IZNOGOUD IS WALKING INCOGNITO, ESCORTED BY HIS FAITHFUL STRONG-ARM MAN WA'AT ALAHF...
THE VILE GRAND VIZIER SEES LITTLE OF THE CITY'S SPLENDOURS, LOST AS HE IS IN HIS OBSESSION...
I HAVE TO FIND A WAY TO GET RID OF CALIPH HAROUN AL PLASSID, SO I CAN BECOME CALIPH IN HIS PLACE...
HEY!!!
WATCH WHERE YOU PUT YOUR FEET!
HUH! I KNOW WHERE I'D LIKE TO PUT MY HAND!
OH YEAH?!
YEAH!!
TOOTLE-OOTLE-OO
POOF
THE CHEEK OF IT!...
?
DID YOU SEE THAT, WA'AT ALAHF?
I SAW, MASTER. HE'S A WIZARD. IT'S NOT LIKE THEY'RE RARE IN BAGHDAD.
LET'S CATCH UP WITH THAT MAN!
OH, MASTER, I CAN SEE WHERE YOU'RE HEADING!
1

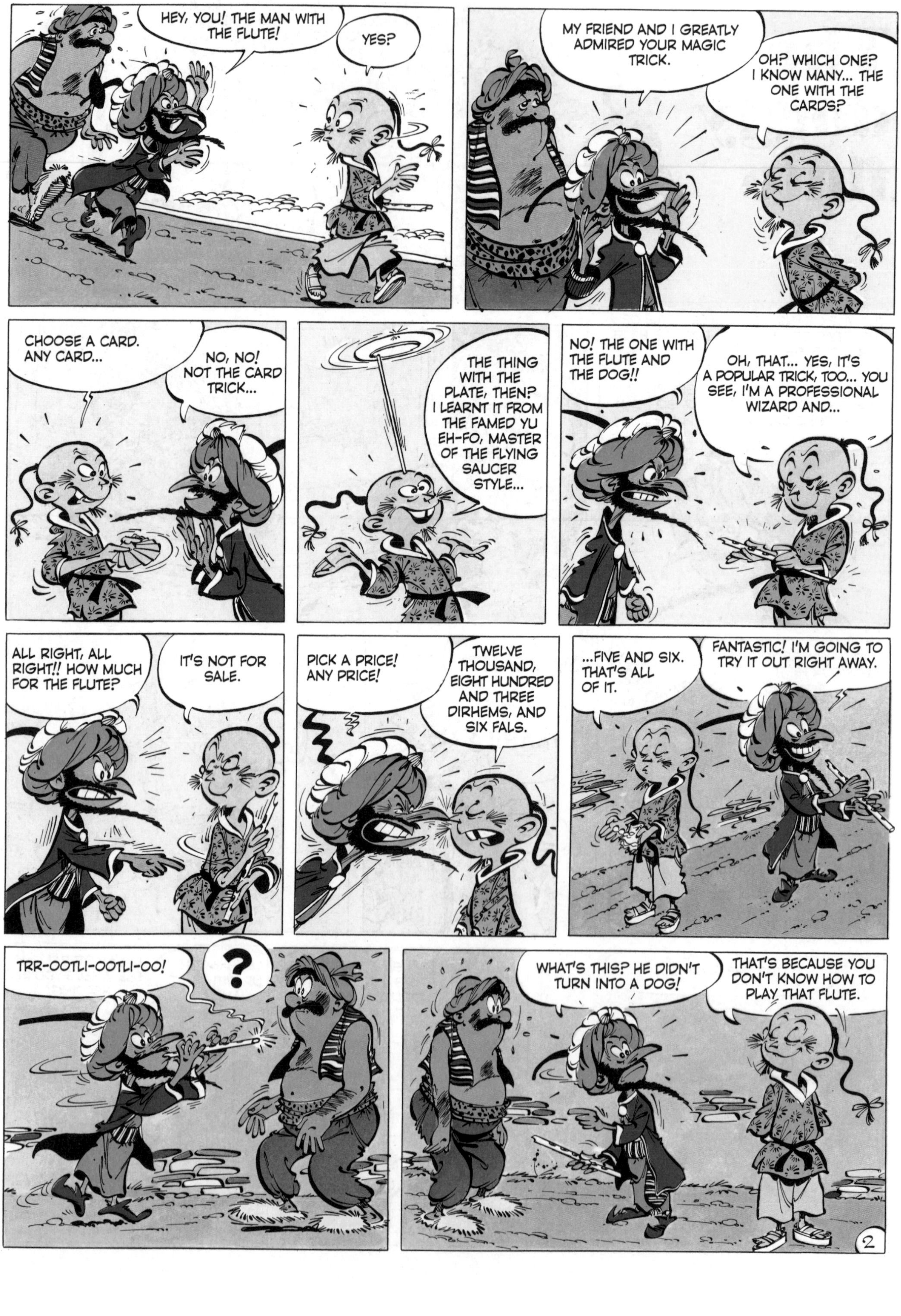
HEY, YOU! THE MAN WITH THE FLUTE!
YES?
MY FRIEND AND I GREATLY ADMIRED YOUR MAGIC TRICK.
OH? WHICH ONE? I KNOW MANY... THE ONE WITH THE CARDS?
CHOOSE A CARD. ANY CARD...
NO, NO! NOT THE CARD TRICK...
THE THING WITH THE PLATE, THEN? I LEARNT IT FROM THE FAMED YU EH-FO, MASTER OF THE FLYING SAUCER STYLE...
NO! THE ONE WITH THE FLUTE AND THE DOG!!
OH, THAT... YES, IT'S A POPULAR TRICK, TOO... YOU SEE, I'M A PROFESSIONAL WIZARD AND...
ALL RIGHT, ALL RIGHT!! HOW MUCH FOR THE FLUTE?
IT'S NOT FOR SALE.
PICK A PRICE! ANY PRICE!
TWELVE THOUSAND, EIGHT HUNDRED AND THREE DIRHEMS, AND SIX FALS.
...FIVE AND SIX. THAT'S ALL OF IT.
FANTASTIC! I'M GOING TO TRY IT OUT RIGHT AWAY.
TRR-OOTLI-OOTLI-OO!
?
WHAT'S THIS? HE DIDN'T TURN INTO A DOG!
THAT'S BECAUSE YOU DON'T KNOW HOW TO PLAY THAT FLUTE.
2

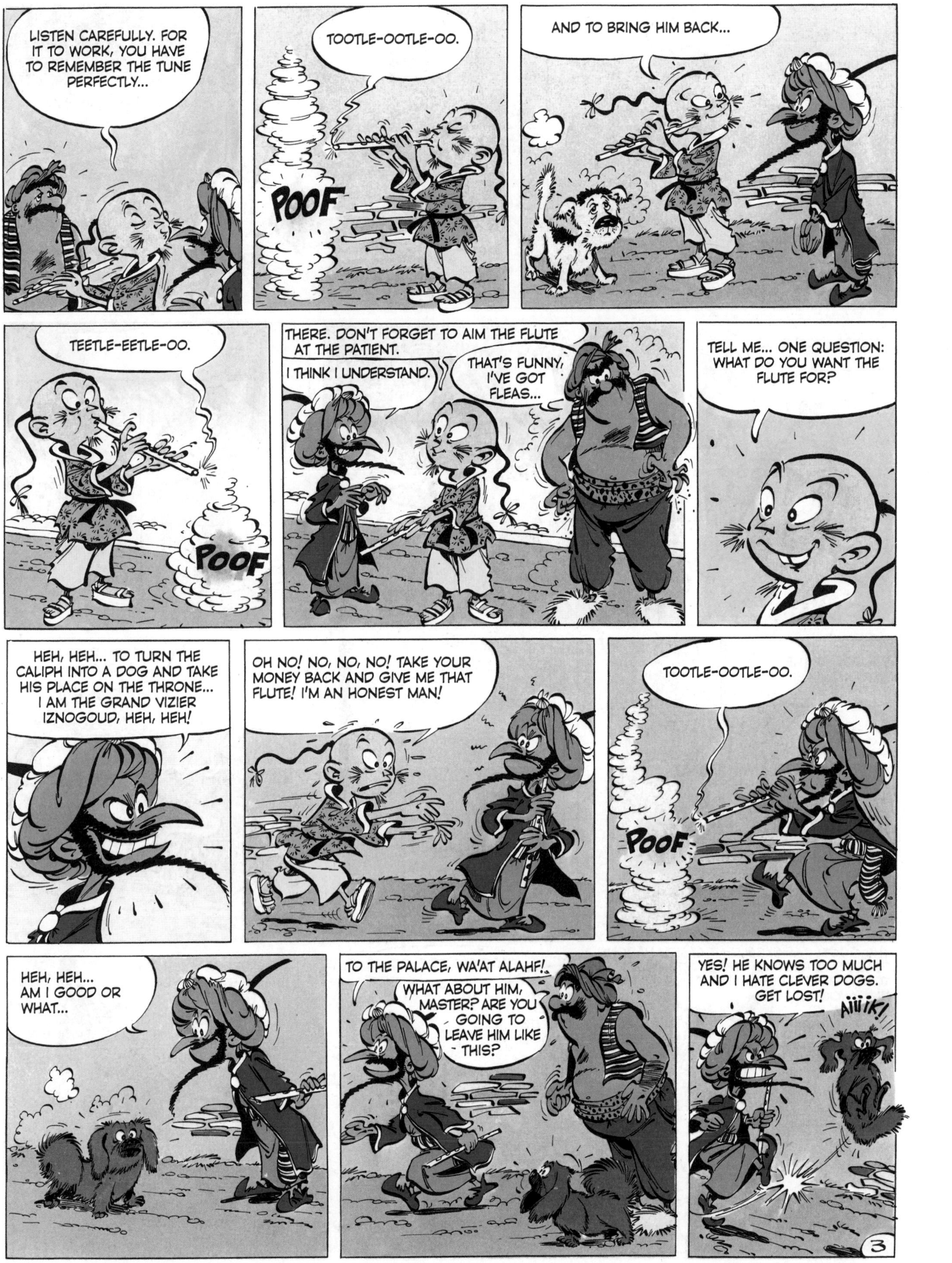
LISTEN CAREFULLY. FOR IT TO WORK, YOU HAVE TO REMEMBER THE TUNE PERFECTLY...
TOOTLE-OOTLE-OO.
POOF
AND TO BRING HIM BACK...
TEETLE-EETLE-OO.
POOF
THERE. DON'T FORGET TO AIM THE FLUTE AT THE PATIENT.
I THINK I UNDERSTAND.
THAT'S FUNNY, I'VE GOT FLEAS...
TELL ME... ONE QUESTION: WHAT DO YOU WANT THE FLUTE FOR?
HEH, HEH... TO TURN THE CALIPH INTO A DOG AND TAKE HIS PLACE ON THE THRONE... I AM THE GRAND VIZIER IZNOGOUD, HEH, HEH!
OH NO! NO, NO, NO! TAKE YOUR MONEY BACK AND GIVE ME THAT FLUTE! I'M AN HONEST MAN!
TOOTLE-OOTLE-OO.
POOF
HEH, HEH... AM I GOOD OR WHAT...
TO THE PALACE, WA'AT ALAHF!
WHAT ABOUT HIM, MASTER? ARE YOU GOING TO LEAVE HIM LIKE THIS?
YES! HE KNOWS TOO MUCH AND I HATE CLEVER DOGS. GET LOST!
AIIIIK!
3

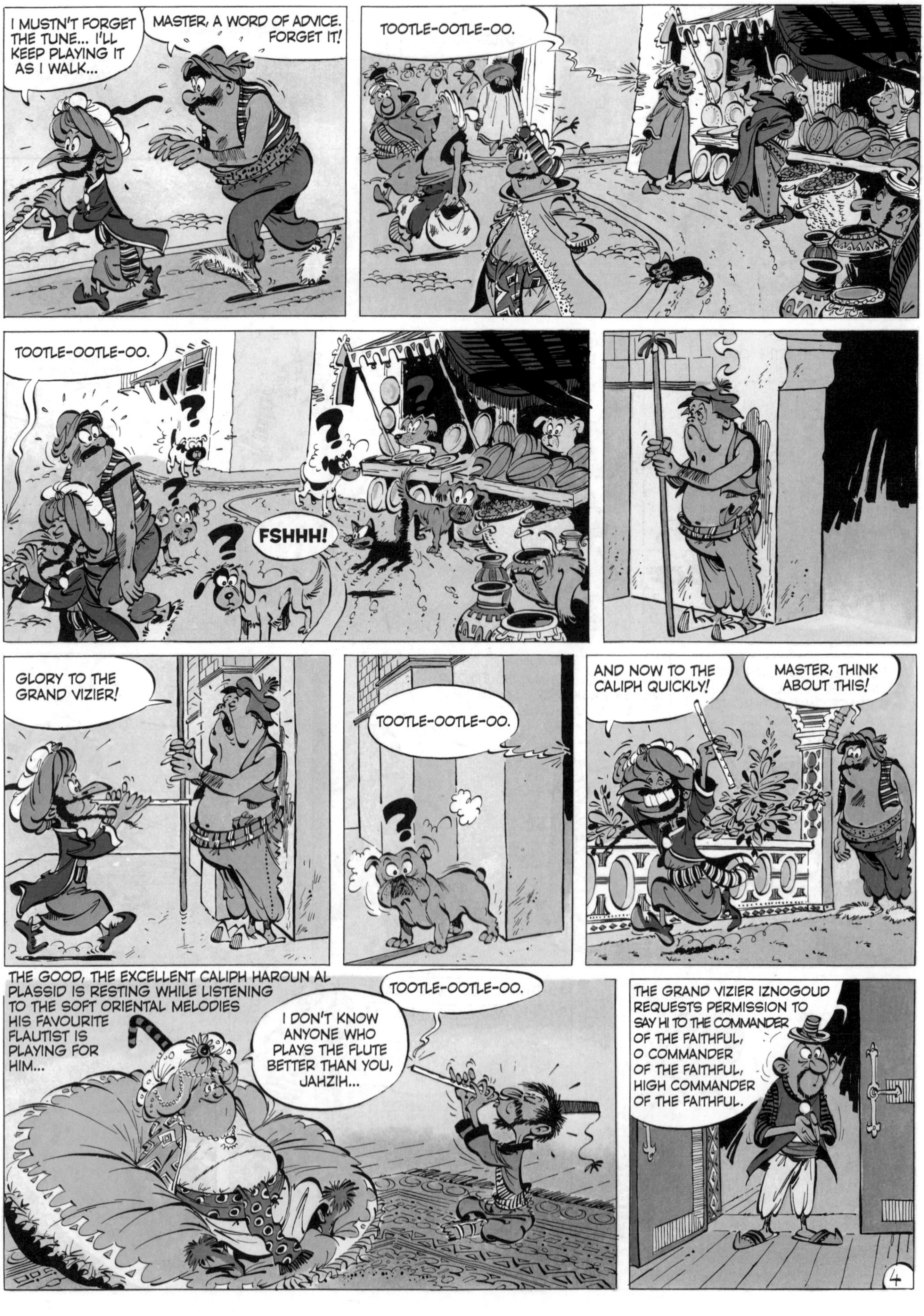
I MUSTN'T FORGET THE TUNE... I'LL KEEP PLAYING IT AS I WALK...
MASTER, A WORD OF ADVICE. FORGET IT!
TOOTLE-OOTLE-OO.
TOOTLE-OOTLE-OO.
FSHHH!
GLORY TO THE GRAND VIZIER!
TOOTLE-OOTLE-OO.
AND NOW TO THE CALIPH QUICKLY!
MASTER, THINK ABOUT THIS!
THE GOOD, THE EXCELLENT CALIPH HAROUN AL PLASSID IS RESTING WHILE LISTENING TO THE SOFT ORIENTAL MELODIES HIS FAVOURITE FLAUTIST IS PLAYING FOR HIM...
TOOTLE-OOTLE-OO.
I DON'T KNOW ANYONE WHO PLAYS THE FLUTE BETTER THAN YOU, JAHZIH...
THE GRAND VIZIER IZNOGOUD REQUESTS PERMISSION TO SAY HI TO THE COMMANDER OF THE FAITHFUL, O COMMANDER OF THE FAITHFUL, HIGH COMMANDER OF THE FAITHFUL.
4

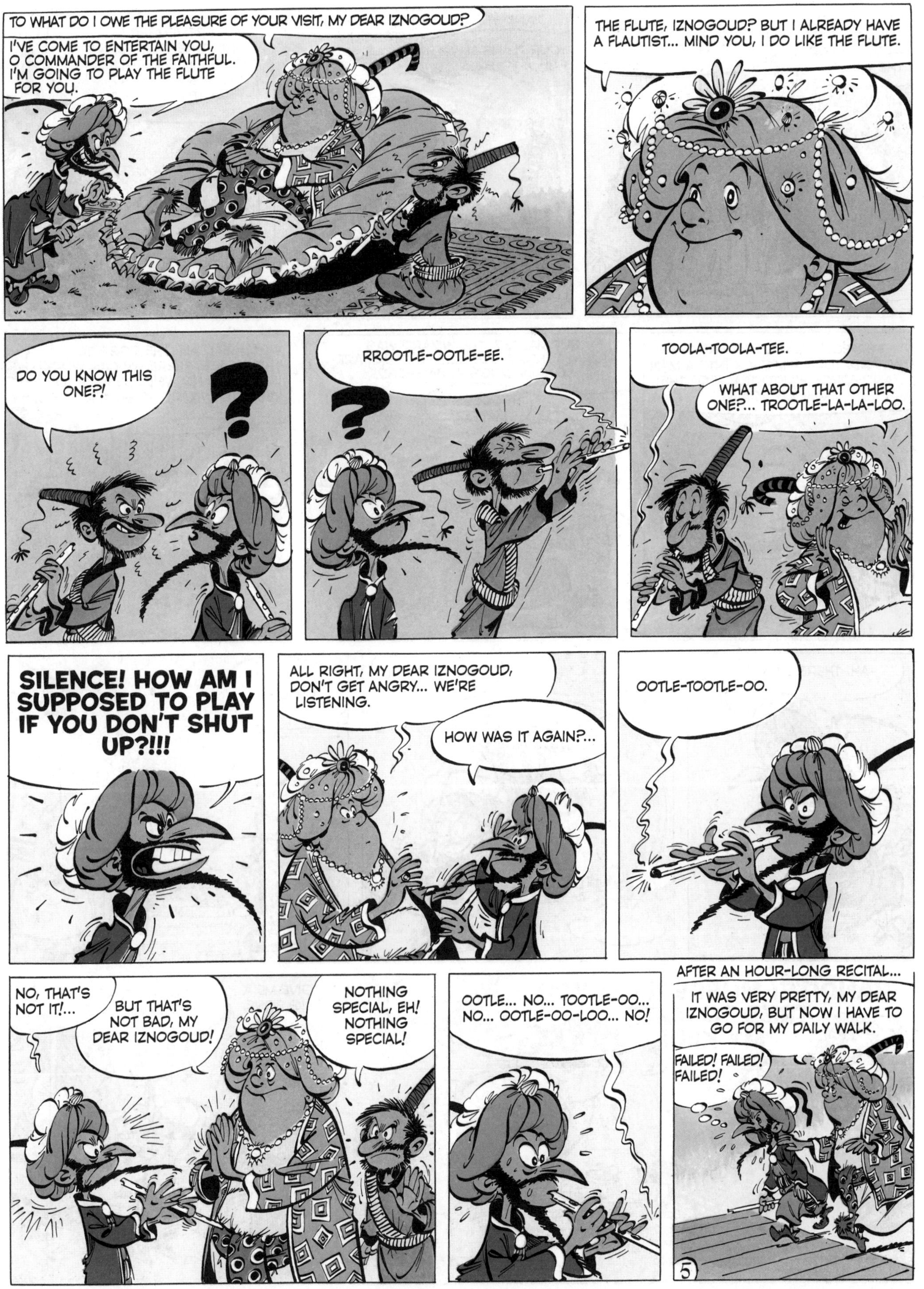
TO WHAT DO I OWE THE PLEASURE OF YOUR VISIT, MY DEAR IZNOGOUD?
I'VE COME TO ENTERTAIN YOU, O COMMANDER OF THE FAITHFUL. I'M GOING TO PLAY THE FLUTE FOR YOU.
THE FLUTE, IZNOGOUD? BUT I ALREADY HAVE A FLAUTIST... MIND YOU, I DO LIKE THE FLUTE.
DO YOU KNOW THIS ONE?!
?
RROOTLE-OOTLE-EE.
?
TOOLA-TOOLA-TEE.
WHAT ABOUT THAT OTHER ONE?... TROOTLE-LA-LA-LOO.
SILENCE! HOW AM I SUPPOSED TO PLAY IF YOU DON'T SHUT UP?!!!
ALL RIGHT, MY DEAR IZNOGOUD, DON'T GET ANGRY... WE'RE LISTENING.
HOW WAS IT AGAIN?...
OOTLE-TOOTLE-OO.
NO, THAT'S NOT IT!...
BUT THAT'S NOT BAD, MY DEAR IZNOGOUD!
NOTHING SPECIAL, EH! NOTHING SPECIAL!
OOTLE... NO... TOOTLE-OO... NO... OOTLE-OO-LOO... NO!
AFTER AN HOUR-LONG RECITAL...
IT WAS VERY PRETTY, MY DEAR IZNOGOUD, BUT NOW I HAVE TO GO FOR MY DAILY WALK.
FAILED! FAILED! FAILED!
5

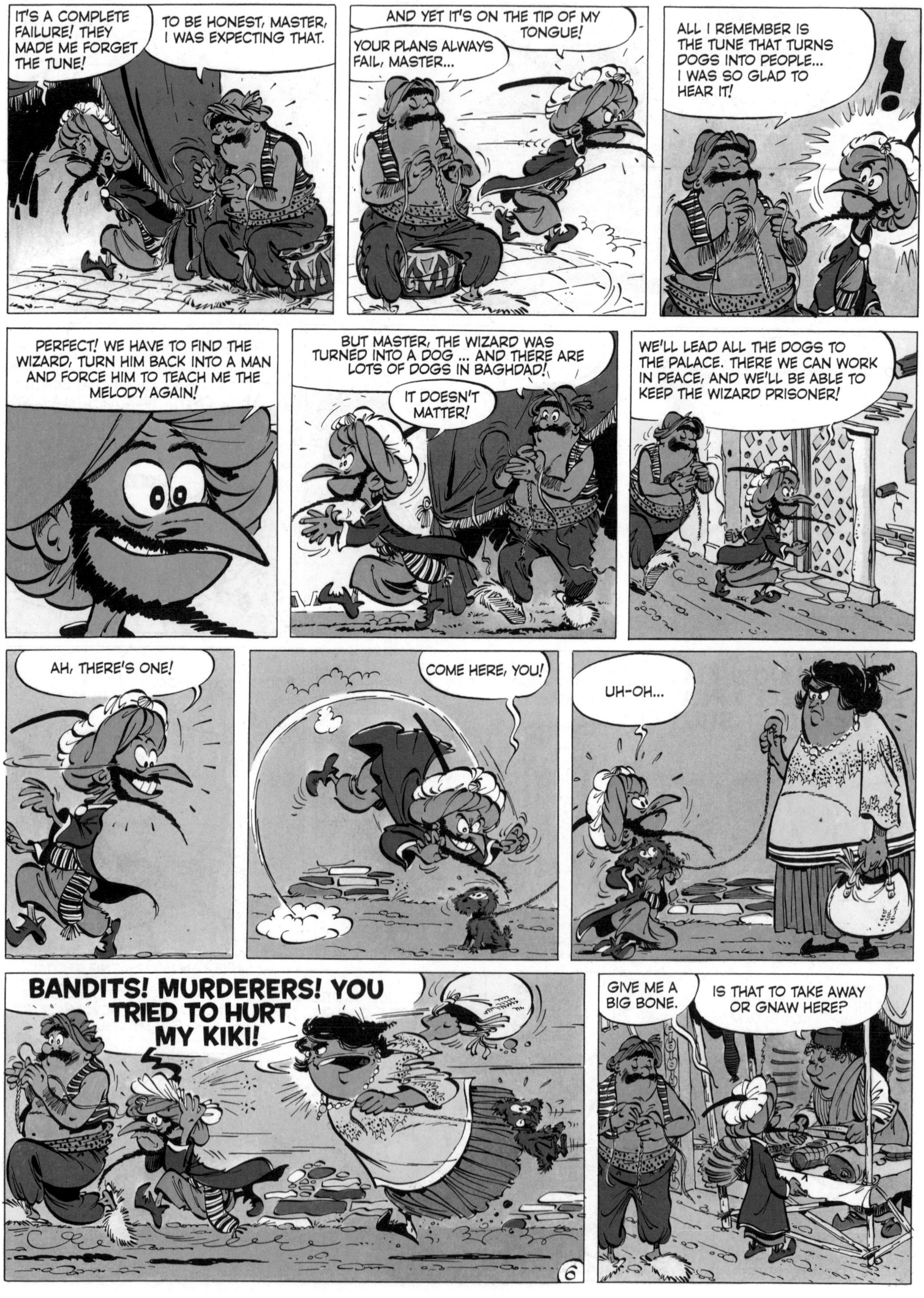
IT'S A COMPLETE FAILURE! THEY MADE ME FORGET THE TUNE!
TO BE HONEST, MASTER, I WAS EXPECTING THAT.
AND YET IT'S ON THE TIP OF MY TONGUE!
YOUR PLANS ALWAYS FAIL, MASTER...
ALL I REMEMBER IS THE TUNE THAT TURNS DOGS INTO PEOPLE... I WAS SO GLAD TO HEAR IT!
!
PERFECT! WE HAVE TO FIND THE WIZARD, TURN HIM BACK INTO A MAN AND FORCE HIM TO TEACH ME THE MELODY AGAIN!
BUT MASTER, THE WIZARD WAS TURNED INTO A DOG ... AND THERE ARE LOTS OF DOGS IN BAGHDAD!
IT DOESN'T MATTER!
WE'LL LEAD ALL THE DOGS TO THE PALACE. THERE WE CAN WORK IN PEACE, AND WE'LL BE ABLE TO KEEP THE WIZARD PRISONER!
AH, THERE'S ONE!
COME HERE, YOU!
UH-OH...
BANDITS! MURDERERS! YOU TRIED TO HURT MY KIKI!
6
GIVE ME A BIG BONE.
IS THAT TO TAKE AWAY OR GNAW HERE?

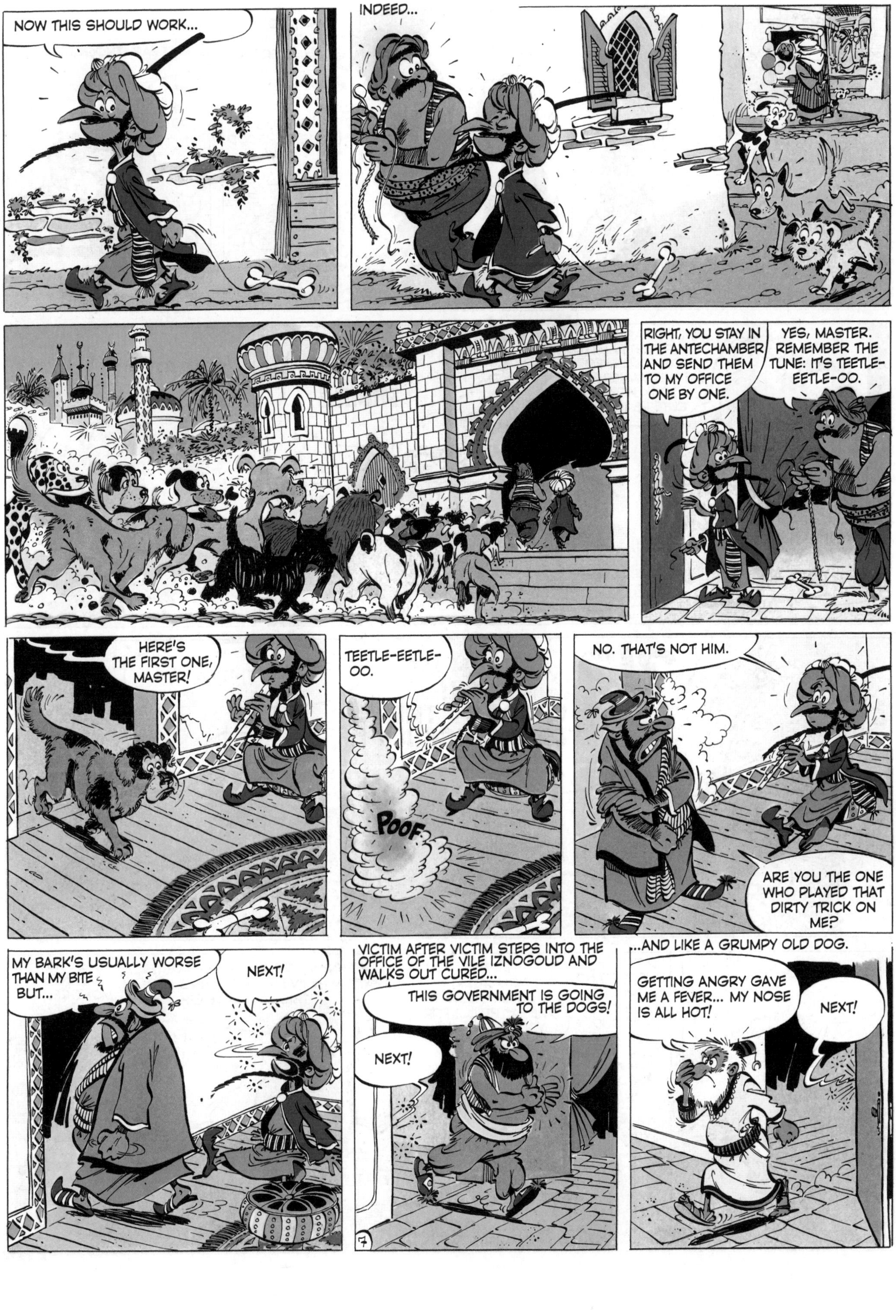
NOW THIS SHOULD WORK...
INDEED...
RIGHT, YOU STAY IN THE ANTECHAMBER AND SEND THEM TO MY OFFICE ONE BY ONE.
YES, MASTER. REMEMBER THE TUNE: IT'S TEETLE-EETLE-OO.
HERE'S THE FIRST ONE, MASTER!
TEETLE-EETLE-OO.
POOF
NO. THAT'S NOT HIM.
ARE YOU THE ONE WHO PLAYED THAT DIRTY TRICK ON ME?
MY BARK'S USUALLY WORSE THAN MY BITE BUT...
NEXT!
VICTIM AFTER VICTIM STEPS INTO THE OFFICE OF THE VILE IZNOGOUD AND WALKS OUT CURED...
THIS GOVERNMENT IS GOING TO THE DOGS!
NEXT!
...AND LIKE A GRUMPY OLD DOG.
GETTING ANGRY GAVE ME A FEVER... MY NOSE IS ALL HOT!
NEXT!

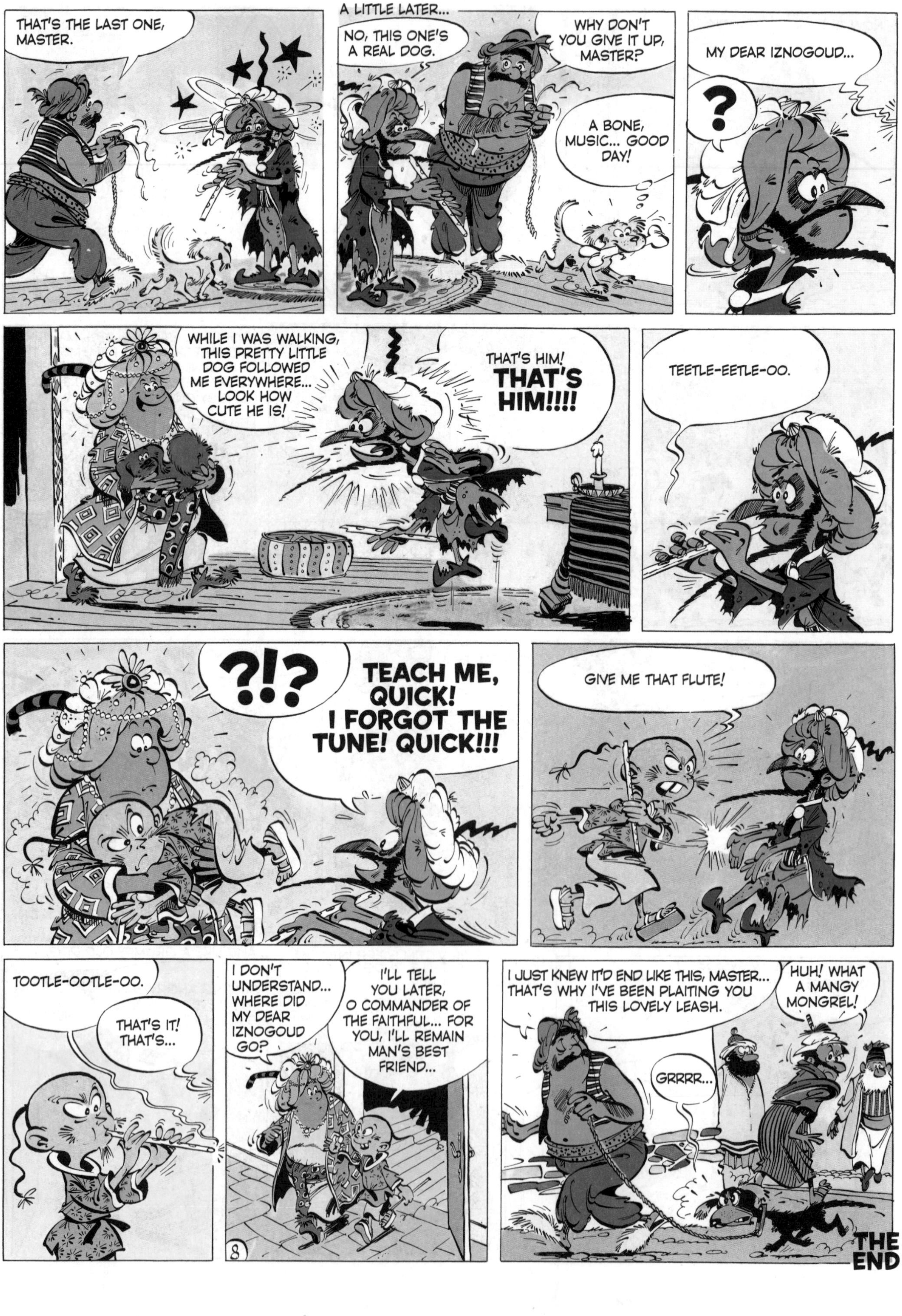
THAT'S THE LAST ONE, MASTER.
A LITTLE LATER...
NO, THIS ONE'S A REAL DOG.
WHY DON'T YOU GIVE IT UP, MASTER?
A BONE, MUSIC... GOOD DAY!
MY DEAR IZNOGOUD...
?
WHILE I WAS WALKING, THIS PRETTY LITTLE DOG FOLLOWED ME EVERYWHERE... LOOK HOW CUTE HE IS!
THAT'S HIM! THAT'S HIM!!!!
TEETLE-EETLE-OO.
?!?
TEACH ME, QUICK! I FORGOT THE TUNE! QUICK!!!
GIVE ME THAT FLUTE!
TOOTLE-OOTLE-OO.
THAT'S IT! THAT'S...
I DON'T UNDERSTAND... WHERE DID MY DEAR IZNOGOUD GO?
I'LL TELL YOU LATER, O COMMANDER OF THE FAITHFUL... FOR YOU, I'LL REMAIN MAN'S BEST FRIEND...
8
I JUST KNEW IT'D END LIKE THIS, MASTER... THAT'S WHY I'VE BEEN PLAITING YOU THIS LOVELY LEASH.
HUH! WHAT A MANGY MONGREL!
GRRRR...
THE END

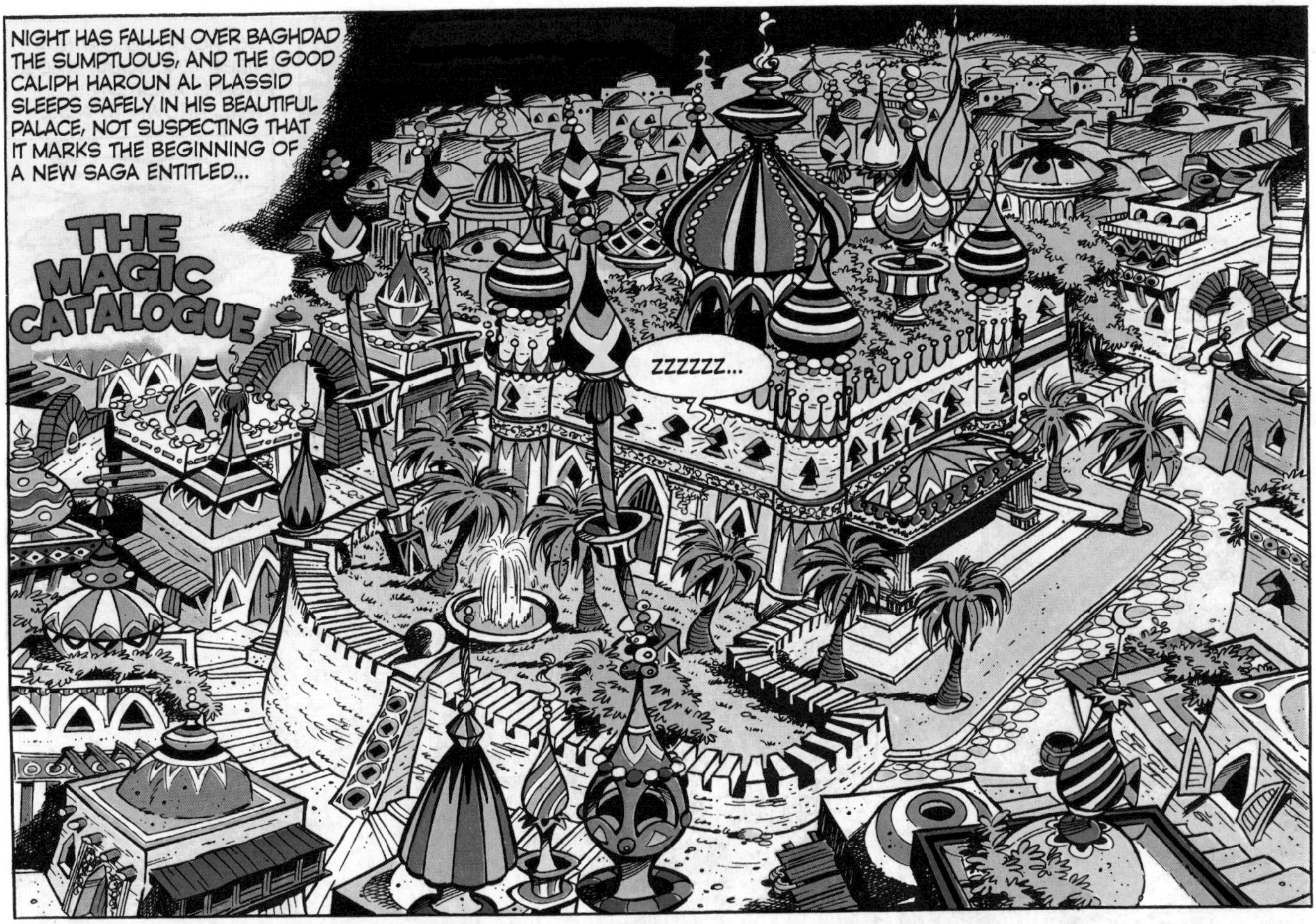
NIGHT HAS FALLEN OVER BAGHDAD THE SUMPTUOUS, AND THE GOOD CALIPH HAROUN AL PLASSID SLEEPS SAFELY IN HIS BEAUTIFUL PALACE, NOT SUSPECTING THAT IT MARKS THE BEGINNING OF A NEW SAGA ENTITLED...
THE MAGIC CATALOGUE
ZZZZZZ...

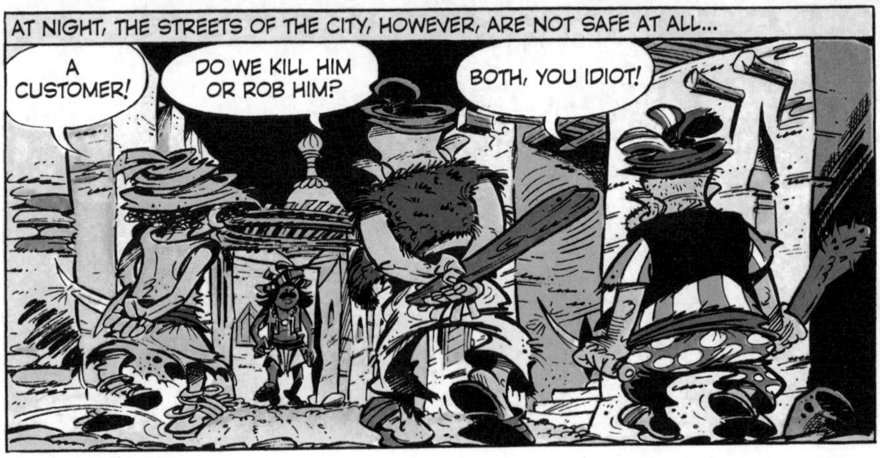
AT NIGHT, THE STREETS OF THE CITY, HOWEVER, ARE NOT SAFE AT ALL...
A CUSTOMER!
DO WE KILL HIM OR ROB HIM?
BOTH, YOU IDIOT!

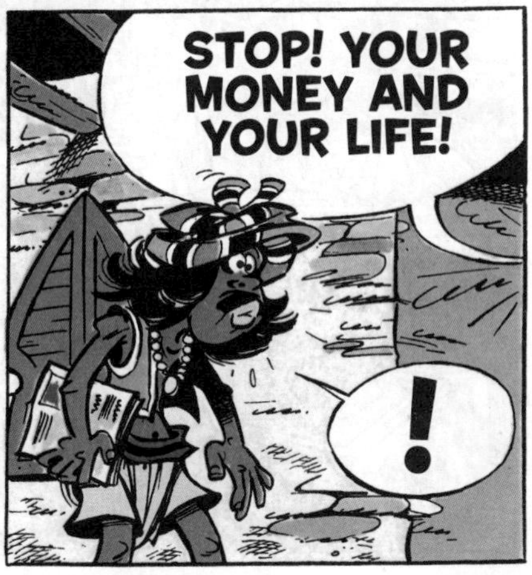
STOP! YOUR MONEY AND YOUR LIFE!
!

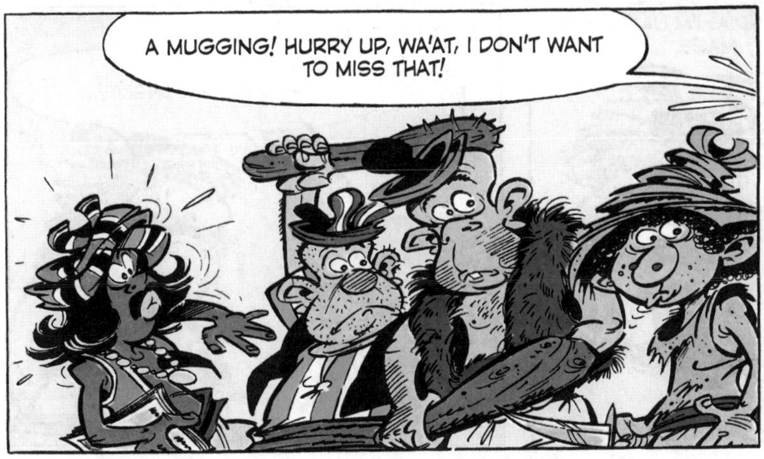
A MUGGING! HURRY UP, WA'AT, I DON'T WANT TO MISS THAT!

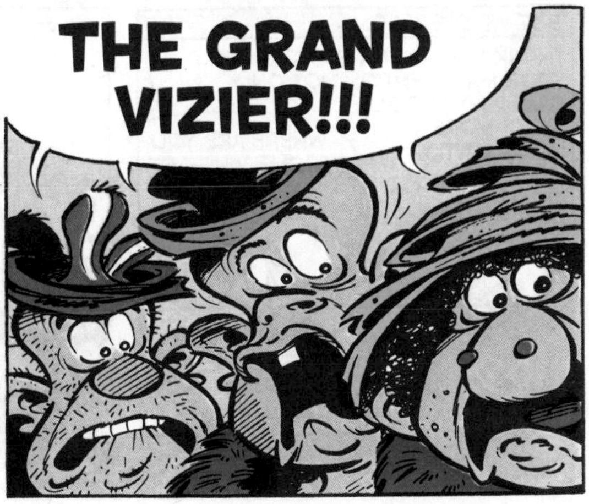
THE GRAND VIZIER!!!

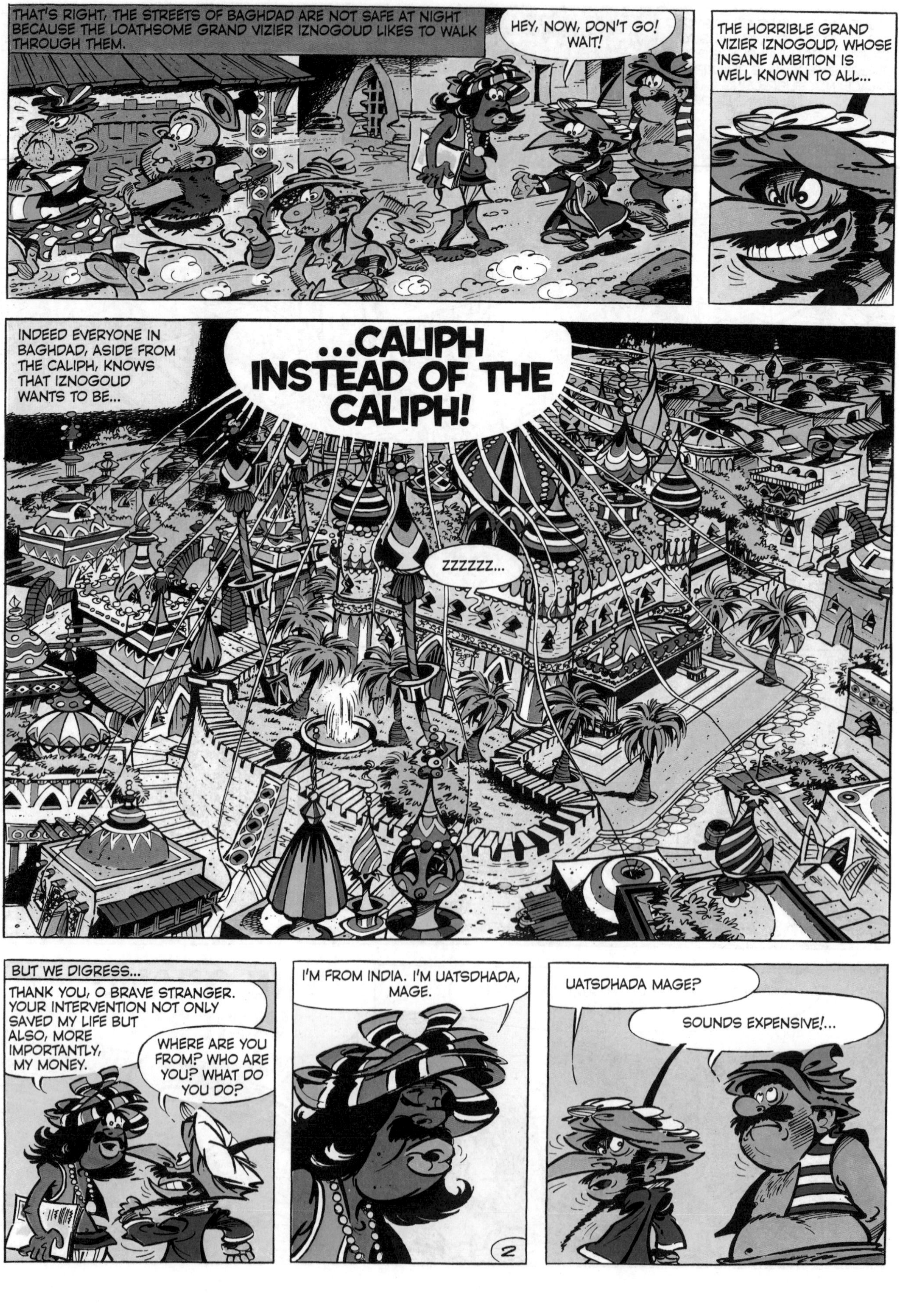

THAT'S RIGHT, THE STREETS OF BAGHDAD ARE NOT SAFE AT NIGHT BECAUSE THE LOATHSOME GRAND VIZIER IZNOGOUD LIKES TO WALK THROUGH THEM.
HEY, NOW, DON'T GO! WAIT!
THE HORRIBLE GRAND VIZIER IZNOGOUD, WHOSE INSANE AMBITION IS WELL KNOWN TO ALL...
INDEED EVERYONE IN BAGHDAD, ASIDE FROM THE CALIPH, KNOWS THAT IZNOGOUD WANTS TO BE...
...CALIPH INSTEAD OF THE CALIPH!
ZZZZZZ...
BUT WE DIGRESS...
THANK YOU, O BRAVE STRANGER. YOUR INTERVENTION NOT ONLY SAVED MY LIFE BUT ALSO, MORE IMPORTANTLY, MY MONEY.
WHERE ARE YOU FROM? WHO ARE YOU? WHAT DO YOU DO?
I'M FROM INDIA. I'M UATSDHADA, MAGE.
UATSDHADA MAGE?
SOUNDS EXPENSIVE!...

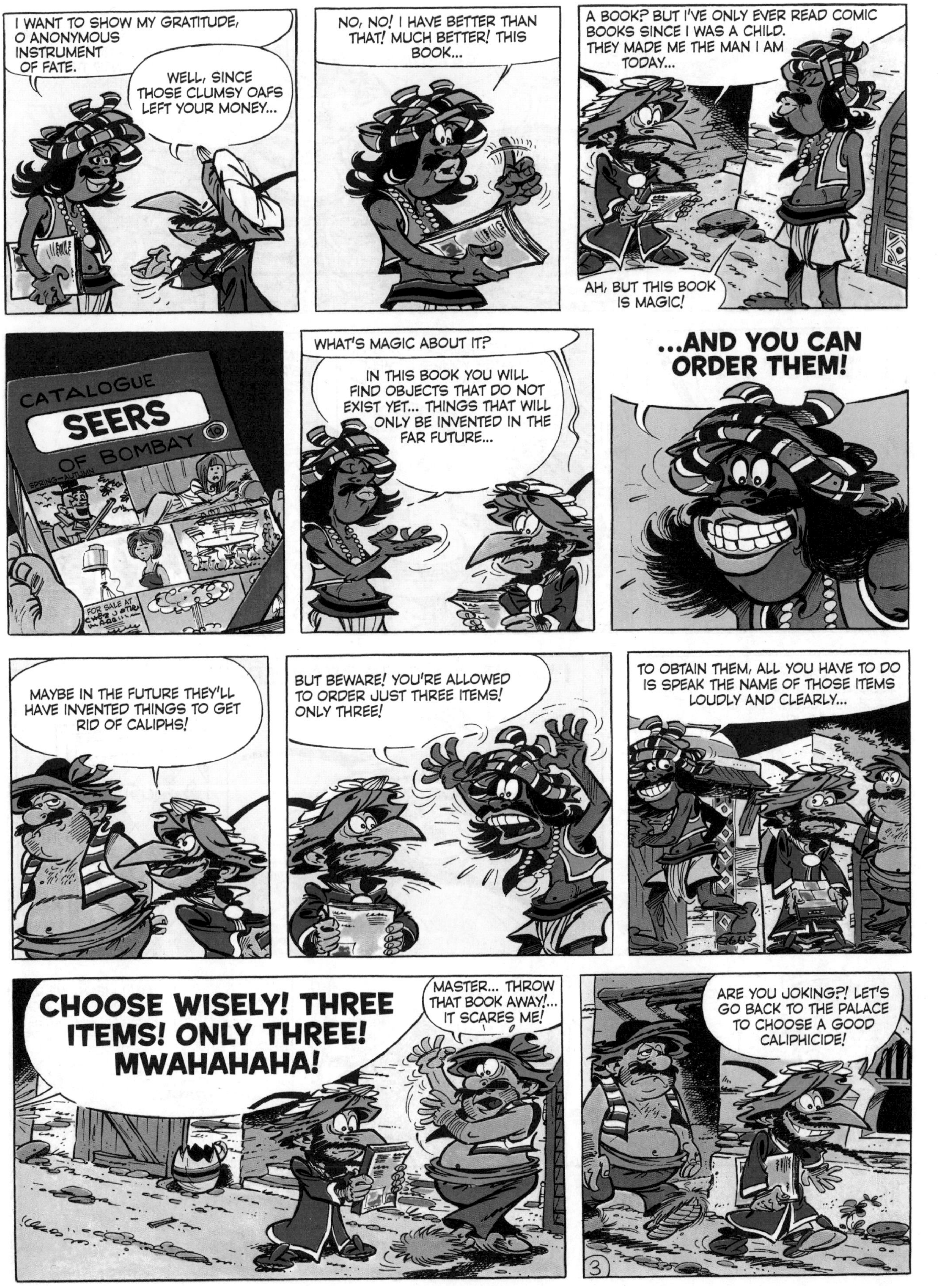
I WANT TO SHOW MY GRATITUDE, O ANONYMOUS INSTRUMENT OF FATE.
WELL, SINCE THOSE CLUMSY OAFS LEFT YOUR MONEY...
NO, NO! I HAVE BETTER THAN THAT! MUCH BETTER! THIS BOOK...
A BOOK? BUT I'VE ONLY EVER READ COMIC BOOKS SINCE I WAS A CHILD. THEY MADE ME THE MAN I AM TODAY...
AH, BUT THIS BOOK IS MAGIC!
CATALOGUE
SEERS
OF BOMBAY
SPRING-AUTUMN
FOR SALE AT
WHAT'S MAGIC ABOUT IT?
IN THIS BOOK YOU WILL FIND OBJECTS THAT DO NOT EXIST YET... THINGS THAT WILL ONLY BE INVENTED IN THE FAR FUTURE...
...AND YOU CAN ORDER THEM!
MAYBE IN THE FUTURE THEY'LL HAVE INVENTED THINGS TO GET RID OF CALIPHS!
BUT BEWARE! YOU'RE ALLOWED TO ORDER JUST THREE ITEMS! ONLY THREE!
TO OBTAIN THEM, ALL YOU HAVE TO DO IS SPEAK THE NAME OF THOSE ITEMS LOUDLY AND CLEARLY...
CHOOSE WISELY! THREE ITEMS! ONLY THREE! MWAHAHAHA!
MASTER... THROW THAT BOOK AWAY!... IT SCARES ME!
ARE YOU JOKING?! LET'S GO BACK TO THE PALACE TO CHOOSE A GOOD CALIPHICIDE!
3

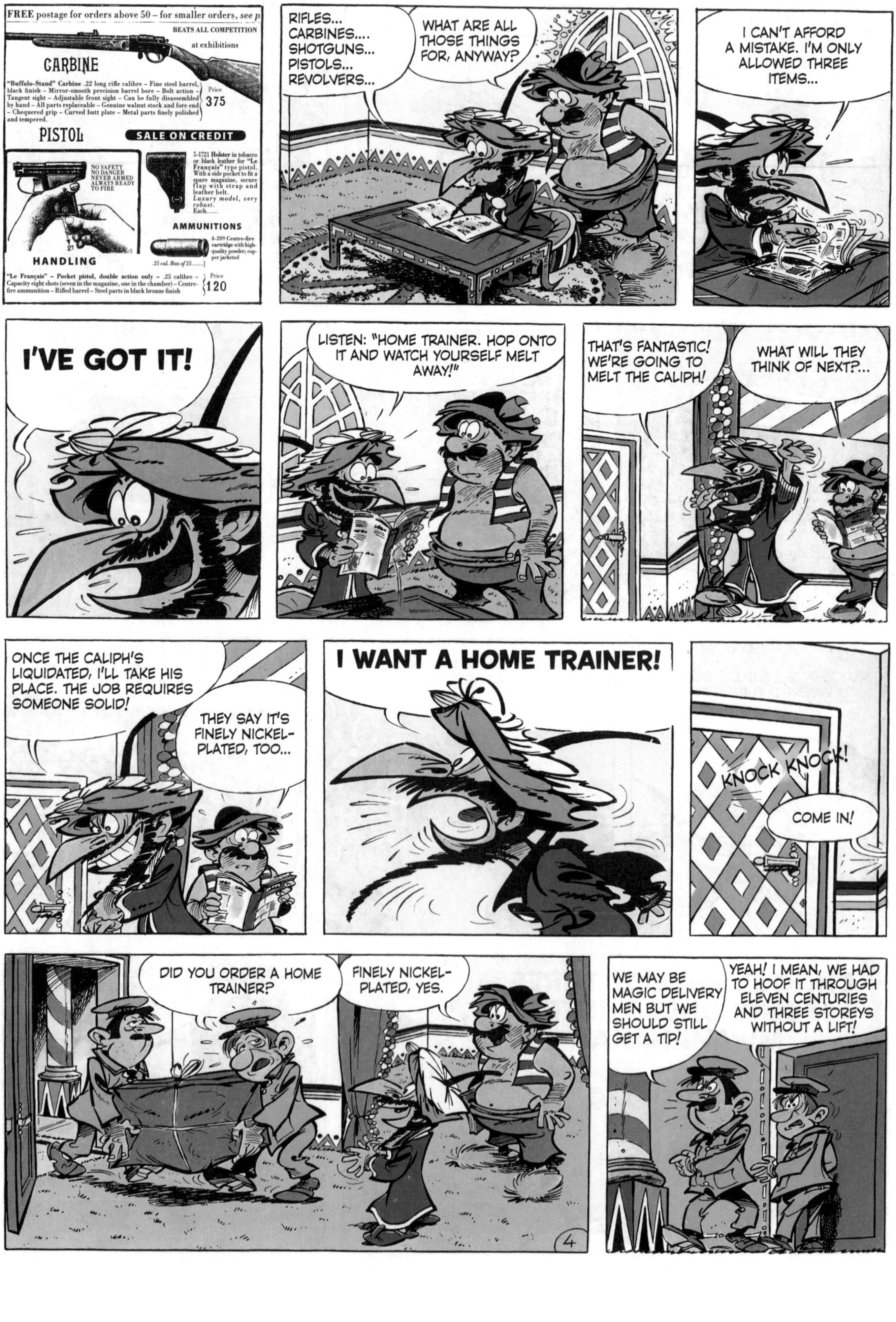
FREE postage for orders above 50 – for smaller orders, see p
BEATS ALL COMPETITION
at exhibitions
CARBINE
"Buffalo-Stand" Carbine .22 long rifle calibre – Fine steel barrel, black finish – Mirror-smooth precision barrel bore – Bolt action – Tangent sight – Adjustable front sight – Can be fully disassembled by hand – All parts replaceable – Genuine walnut stock and fore end – Chequered grip – Curved butt plate – Metal parts finely polished and tempered.
Price 375
PISTOL
SALE ON CREDIT
NO SAFETY NO DANGER NEVER ARMED ALWAYS READY TO FIRE
HANDLING
5-1721 Holster in tobacco or black leather for "Le Français" type pistol. With a side pocket to fit a spare magazine, secure flap with strap and leather belt. Luxury model, very robust. Each......
AMMUNITIONS
4-209 Centre-fire cartridge with high-quality powder; copper jacketed
.25 cal. Box of 25.......
"Le Français" – Pocket pistol, double action only – .25 calibre – Capacity eight shots (seven in the magazine, one in the chamber) – Centre-fire ammunition – Rifled barrel – Steel parts in black bronze finish
Price 120
RIFLES... CARBINES.... SHOTGUNS... PISTOLS... REVOLVERS...
WHAT ARE ALL THOSE THINGS FOR, ANYWAY?
I CAN'T AFFORD A MISTAKE. I'M ONLY ALLOWED THREE ITEMS...
I'VE GOT IT!
LISTEN: "HOME TRAINER. HOP ONTO IT AND WATCH YOURSELF MELT AWAY!"
THAT'S FANTASTIC! WE'RE GOING TO MELT THE CALIPH!
WHAT WILL THEY THINK OF NEXT?...
ONCE THE CALIPH'S LIQUIDATED, I'LL TAKE HIS PLACE. THE JOB REQUIRES SOMEONE SOLID!
THEY SAY IT'S FINELY NICKEL-PLATED, TOO...
I WANT A HOME TRAINER!
KNOCK KNOCK!
COME IN!
DID YOU ORDER A HOME TRAINER?
FINELY NICKEL-PLATED, YES.
4
WE MAY BE MAGIC DELIVERY MEN BUT WE SHOULD STILL GET A TIP!
YEAH! I MEAN, WE HAD TO HOOF IT THROUGH ELEVEN CENTURIES AND THREE STOREYS WITHOUT A LIFT!

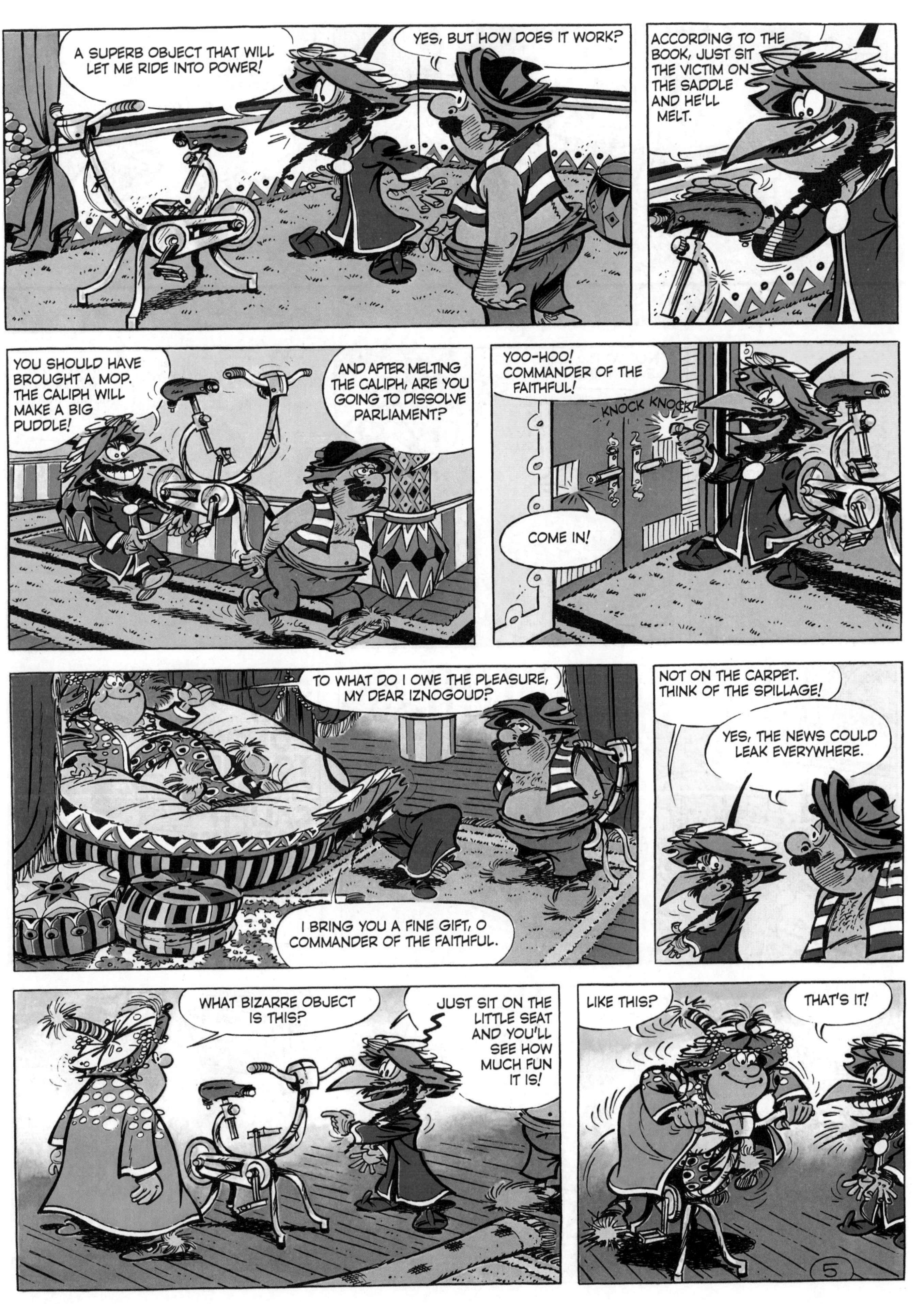
A SUPERB OBJECT THAT WILL LET ME RIDE INTO POWER!
YES, BUT HOW DOES IT WORK?
ACCORDING TO THE BOOK, JUST SIT THE VICTIM ON THE SADDLE AND HE'LL MELT.
YOU SHOULD HAVE BROUGHT A MOP. THE CALIPH WILL MAKE A BIG PUDDLE!
AND AFTER MELTING THE CALIPH, ARE YOU GOING TO DISSOLVE PARLIAMENT?
YOO-HOO! COMMANDER OF THE FAITHFUL!
KNOCK KNOCK
COME IN!
TO WHAT DO I OWE THE PLEASURE, MY DEAR IZNOGOUD?
I BRING YOU A FINE GIFT, O COMMANDER OF THE FAITHFUL.
NOT ON THE CARPET. THINK OF THE SPILLAGE!
YES, THE NEWS COULD LEAK EVERYWHERE.
WHAT BIZARRE OBJECT IS THIS?
JUST SIT ON THE LITTLE SEAT AND YOU'LL SEE HOW MUCH FUN IT IS!
LIKE THIS?
THAT'S IT!
5

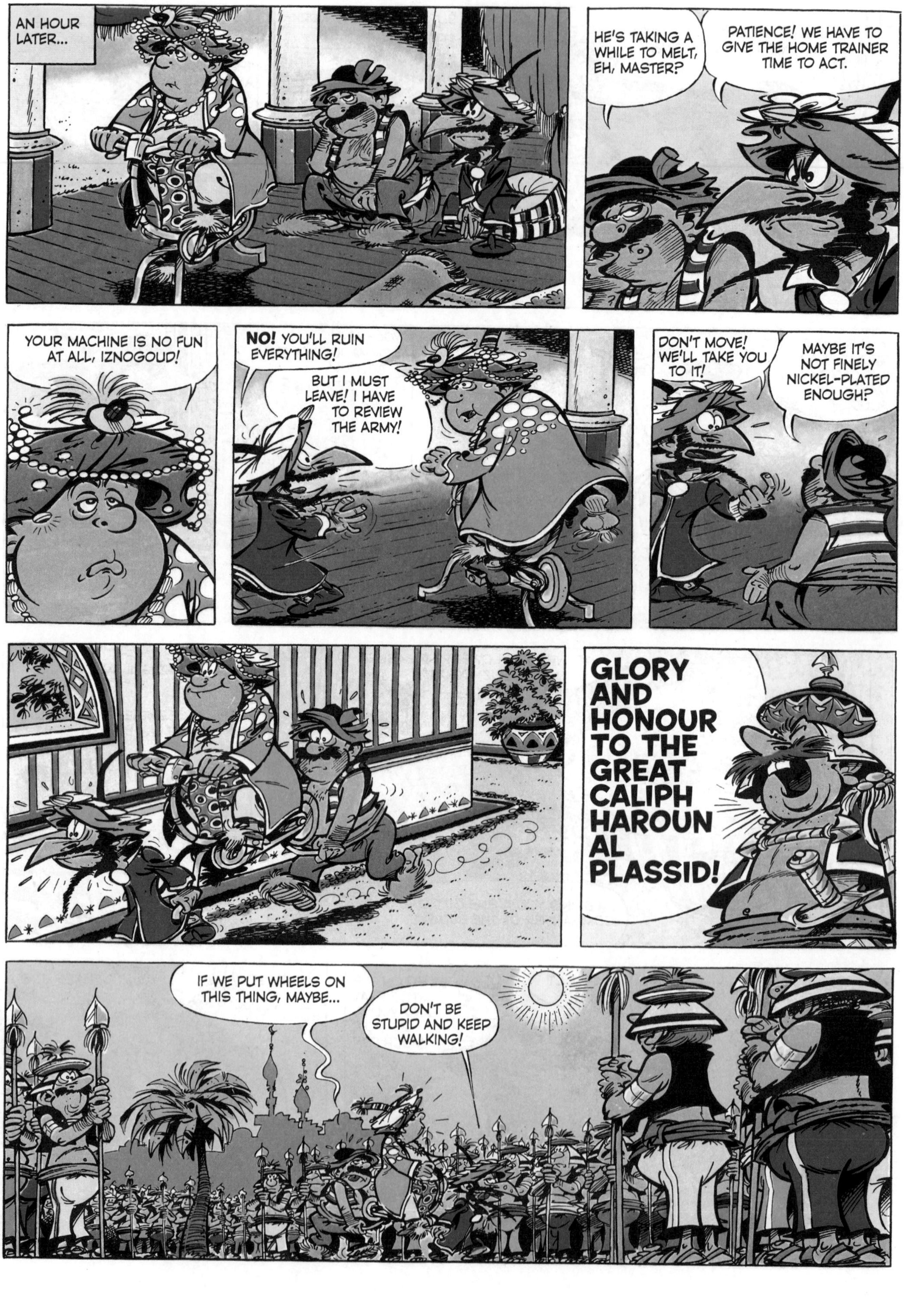
AN HOUR LATER...
HE'S TAKING A WHILE TO MELT, EH, MASTER?
PATIENCE! WE HAVE TO GIVE THE HOME TRAINER TIME TO ACT.
YOUR MACHINE IS NO FUN AT ALL, IZNOGOUD!
BUT I MUST LEAVE! I HAVE TO REVIEW THE ARMY!
NO! YOU'LL RUIN EVERYTHING!
DON'T MOVE! WE'LL TAKE YOU TO IT!
MAYBE IT'S NOT FINELY NICKEL-PLATED ENOUGH?
GLORY AND HONOUR TO THE GREAT CALIPH HAROUN AL PLASSID!
IF WE PUT WHEELS ON THIS THING, MAYBE...
DON'T BE STUPID AND KEEP WALKING!

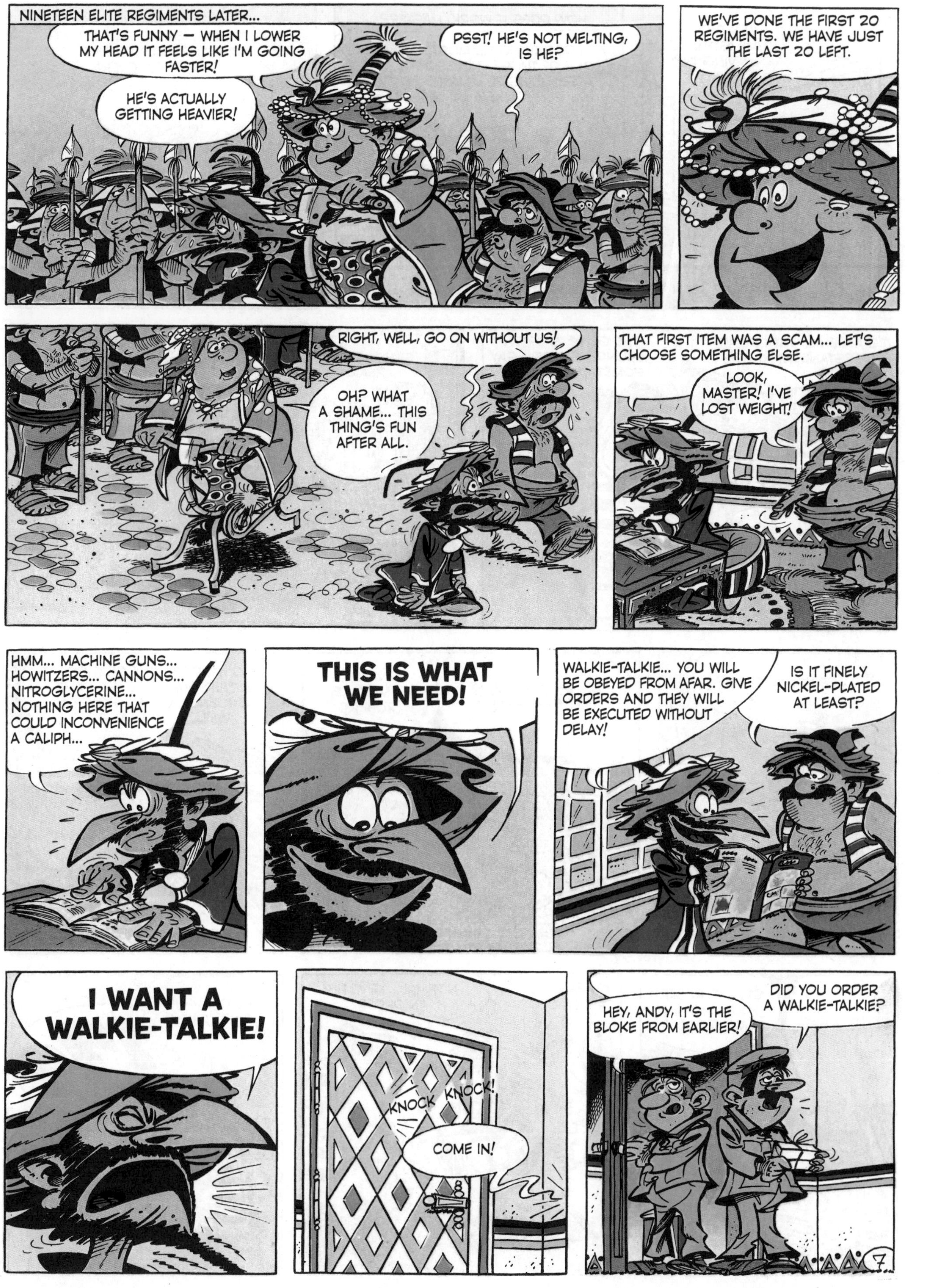
NINETEEN ELITE REGIMENTS LATER...
THAT'S FUNNY — WHEN I LOWER MY HEAD IT FEELS LIKE I'M GOING FASTER!
HE'S ACTUALLY GETTING HEAVIER!
PSST! HE'S NOT MELTING, IS HE?
WE'VE DONE THE FIRST 20 REGIMENTS. WE HAVE JUST THE LAST 20 LEFT.
RIGHT, WELL, GO ON WITHOUT US!
OH? WHAT A SHAME... THIS THING'S FUN AFTER ALL.
THAT FIRST ITEM WAS A SCAM... LET'S CHOOSE SOMETHING ELSE.
LOOK, MASTER! I'VE LOST WEIGHT!
HMM... MACHINE GUNS... HOWITZERS... CANNONS... NITROGLYCERINE... NOTHING HERE THAT COULD INCONVENIENCE A CALIPH...
THIS IS WHAT WE NEED!
WALKIE-TALKIE... YOU WILL BE OBEYED FROM AFAR. GIVE ORDERS AND THEY WILL BE EXECUTED WITHOUT DELAY!
IS IT FINELY NICKEL-PLATED AT LEAST?
I WANT A WALKIE-TALKIE!
KNOCK KNOCK!
COME IN!
DID YOU ORDER A WALKIE-TALKIE?
HEY, ANDY, IT'S THE BLOKE FROM EARLIER!
7

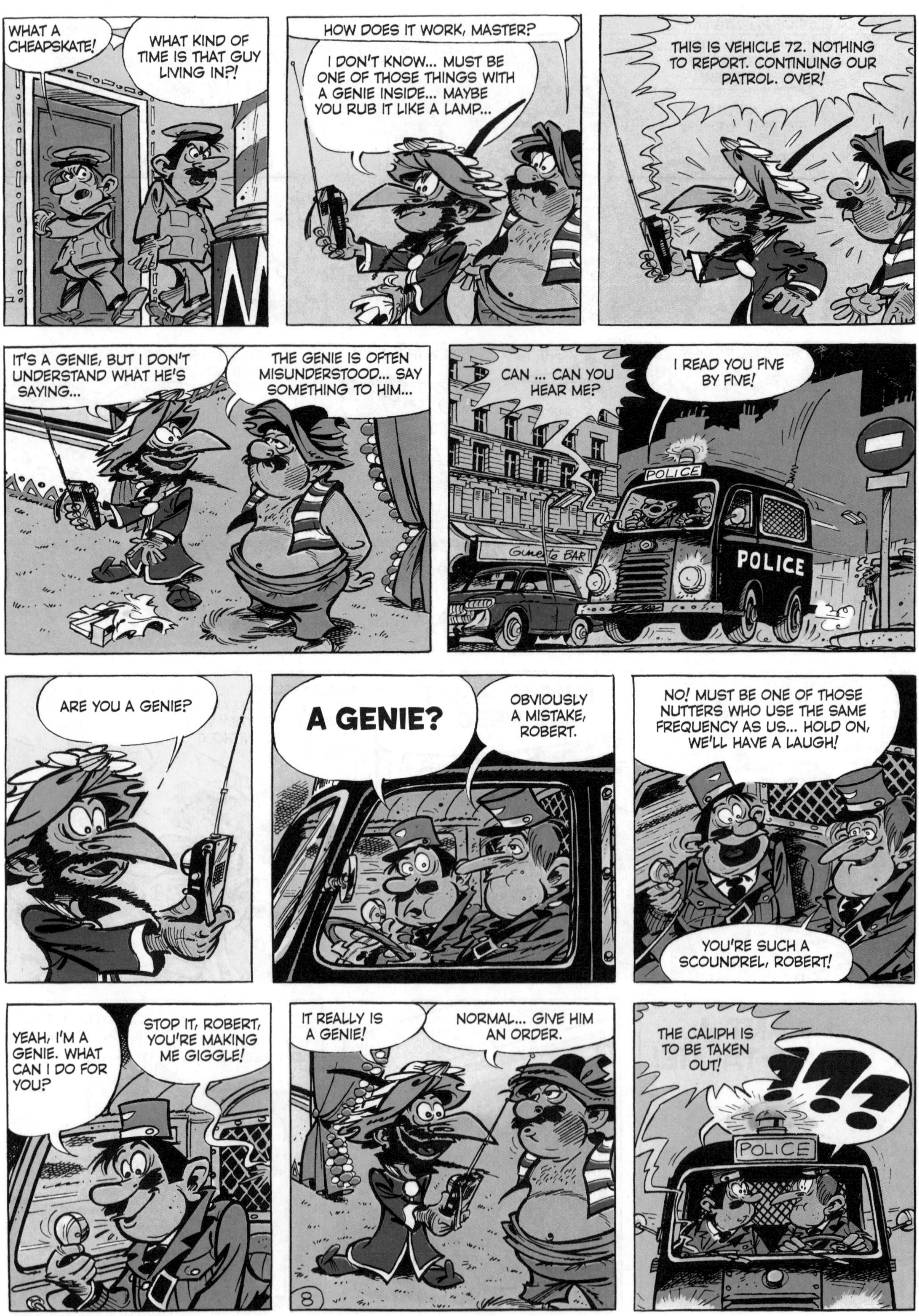
WHAT A CHEAPSKATE!
WHAT KIND OF TIME IS THAT GUY LIVING IN?!
HOW DOES IT WORK, MASTER?
I DON'T KNOW... MUST BE ONE OF THOSE THINGS WITH A GENIE INSIDE... MAYBE YOU RUB IT LIKE A LAMP...
THIS IS VEHICLE 72. NOTHING TO REPORT. CONTINUING OUR PATROL. OVER!
IT'S A GENIE, BUT I DON'T UNDERSTAND WHAT HE'S SAYING...
THE GENIE IS OFTEN MISUNDERSTOOD... SAY SOMETHING TO HIM...
CAN ... CAN YOU HEAR ME?
I READ YOU FIVE BY FIVE!
POLICE
POLICE
ARE YOU A GENIE?
A GENIE?
OBVIOUSLY A MISTAKE, ROBERT.
NO! MUST BE ONE OF THOSE NUTTERS WHO USE THE SAME FREQUENCY AS US... HOLD ON, WE'LL HAVE A LAUGH!
YOU'RE SUCH A SCOUNDREL, ROBERT!
YEAH, I'M A GENIE. WHAT CAN I DO FOR YOU?
STOP IT, ROBERT, YOU'RE MAKING ME GIGGLE!
IT REALLY IS A GENIE!
NORMAL... GIVE HIM AN ORDER.
THE CALIPH IS TO BE TAKEN OUT!
?!?
POLICE

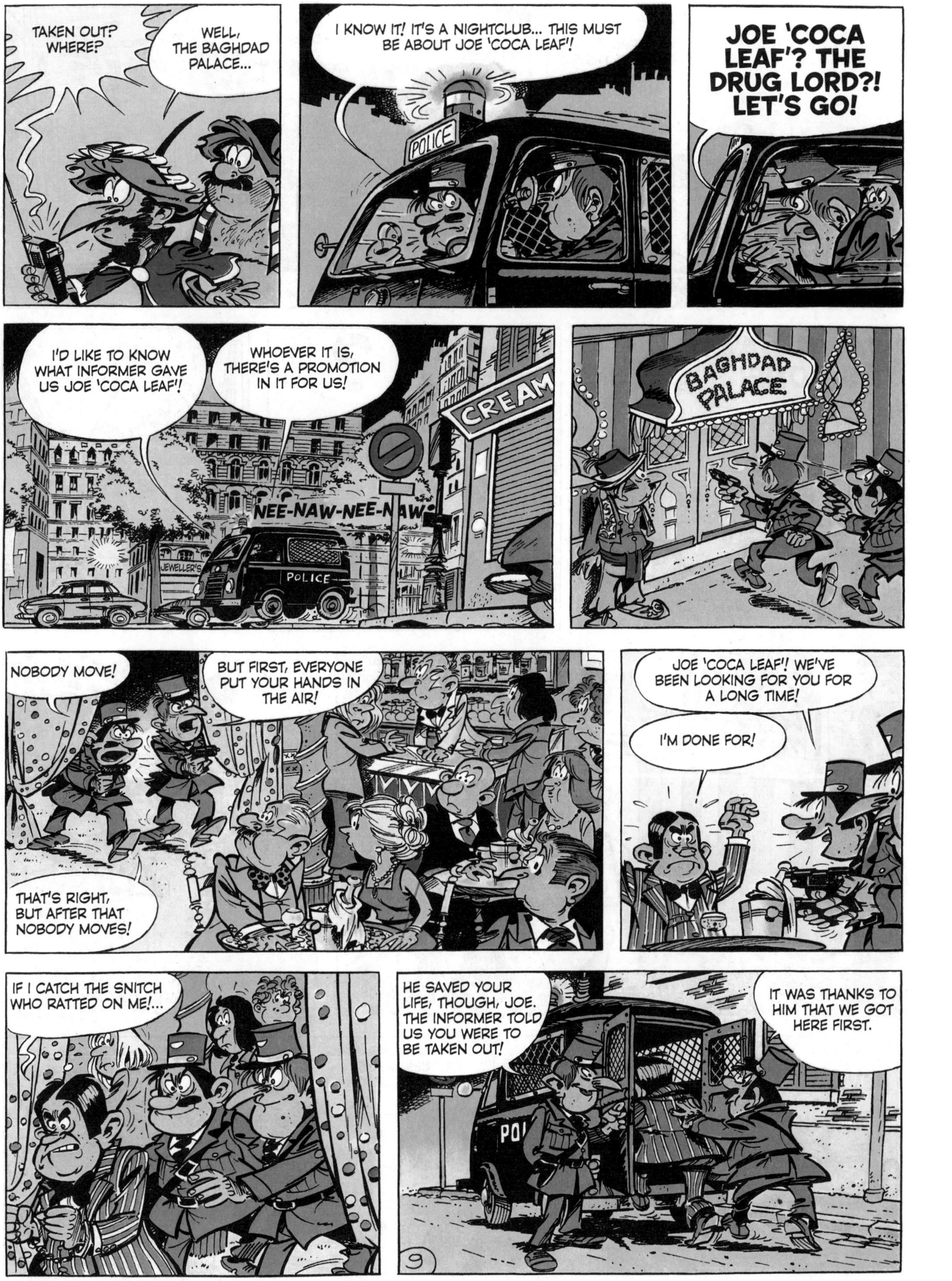
TAKEN OUT? WHERE?
WELL, THE BAGHDAD PALACE...
I KNOW IT! IT'S A NIGHTCLUB... THIS MUST BE ABOUT JOE 'COCA LEAF'!
POLICE
JOE 'COCA LEAF'? THE DRUG LORD?! LET'S GO!
I'D LIKE TO KNOW WHAT INFORMER GAVE US JOE 'COCA LEAF'!
WHOEVER IT IS, THERE'S A PROMOTION IN IT FOR US!
CREAM
NEE-NAW-NEE-NAW
JEWELLER'S
POLICE
BAGHDAD PALACE
NOBODY MOVE!
BUT FIRST, EVERYONE PUT YOUR HANDS IN THE AIR!
THAT'S RIGHT, BUT AFTER THAT NOBODY MOVES!
JOE 'COCA LEAF'! WE'VE BEEN LOOKING FOR YOU FOR A LONG TIME!
I'M DONE FOR!
IF I CATCH THE SNITCH WHO RATTED ON ME!...
HE SAVED YOUR LIFE, THOUGH, JOE. THE INFORMER TOLD US YOU WERE TO BE TAKEN OUT!
IT WAS THANKS TO HIM THAT WE GOT HERE FIRST.
POI
9

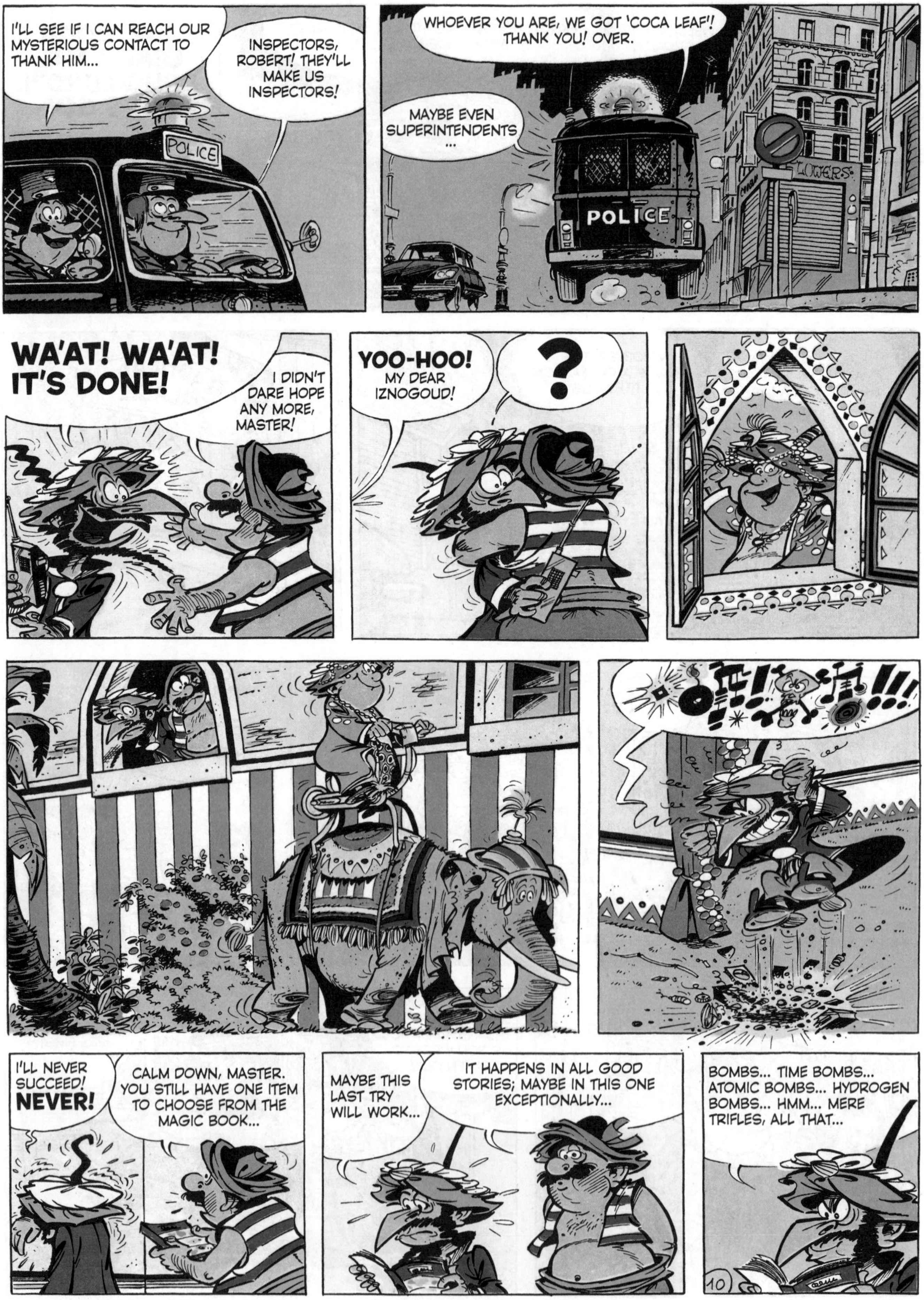

I'LL SEE IF I CAN REACH OUR MYSTERIOUS CONTACT TO THANK HIM...
INSPECTORS, ROBERT! THEY'LL MAKE US INSPECTORS!
POLICE
WHOEVER YOU ARE, WE GOT 'COCA LEAF'! THANK YOU! OVER.
MAYBE EVEN SUPERINTENDENTS ...
POLICE
WA'AT! WA'AT! IT'S DONE!
I DIDN'T DARE HOPE ANY MORE, MASTER!
YOO-HOO! MY DEAR IZNOGOUD!
?
I'LL NEVER SUCCEED! NEVER!
CALM DOWN, MASTER. YOU STILL HAVE ONE ITEM TO CHOOSE FROM THE MAGIC BOOK...
MAYBE THIS LAST TRY WILL WORK...
IT HAPPENS IN ALL GOOD STORIES; MAYBE IN THIS ONE EXCEPTIONALLY...
BOMBS... TIME BOMBS... ATOMIC BOMBS... HYDROGEN BOMBS... HMM... MERE TRIFLES, ALL THAT...

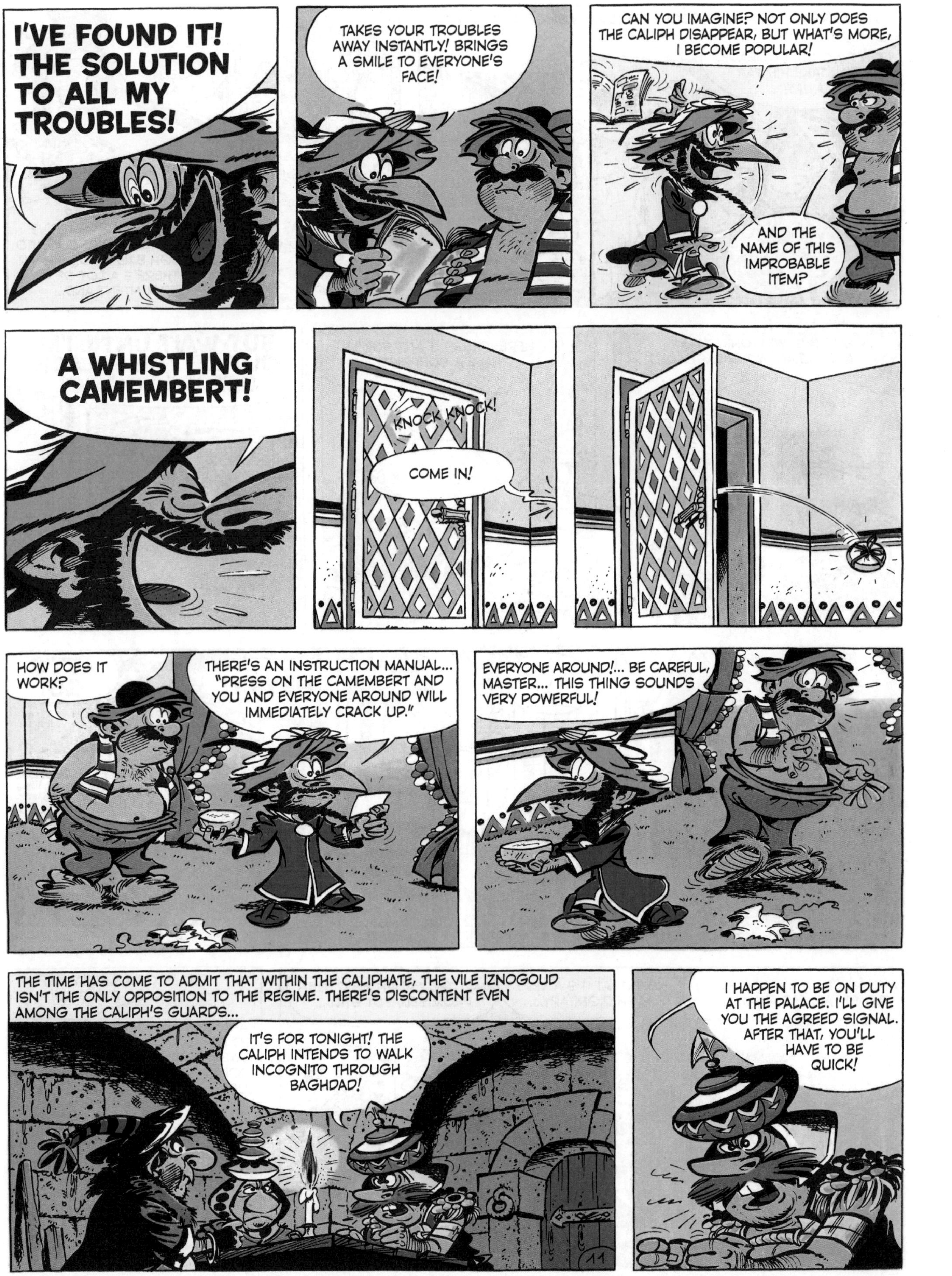
I'VE FOUND IT! THE SOLUTION TO ALL MY TROUBLES!
TAKES YOUR TROUBLES AWAY INSTANTLY! BRINGS A SMILE TO EVERYONE'S FACE!
CAN YOU IMAGINE? NOT ONLY DOES THE CALIPH DISAPPEAR, BUT WHAT'S MORE, I BECOME POPULAR!
AND THE NAME OF THIS IMPROBABLE ITEM?
A WHISTLING CAMEMBERT!
KNOCK KNOCK!
COME IN!
HOW DOES IT WORK?
THERE'S AN INSTRUCTION MANUAL... "PRESS ON THE CAMEMBERT AND YOU AND EVERYONE AROUND WILL IMMEDIATELY CRACK UP."
EVERYONE AROUND!... BE CAREFUL, MASTER... THIS THING SOUNDS VERY POWERFUL!
THE TIME HAS COME TO ADMIT THAT WITHIN THE CALIPHATE, THE VILE IZNOGOUD ISN'T THE ONLY OPPOSITION TO THE REGIME. THERE'S DISCONTENT EVEN AMONG THE CALIPH'S GUARDS...
IT'S FOR TONIGHT! THE CALIPH INTENDS TO WALK INCOGNITO THROUGH BAGHDAD!
I HAPPEN TO BE ON DUTY AT THE PALACE. I'LL GIVE YOU THE AGREED SIGNAL. AFTER THAT, YOU'LL HAVE TO BE QUICK!

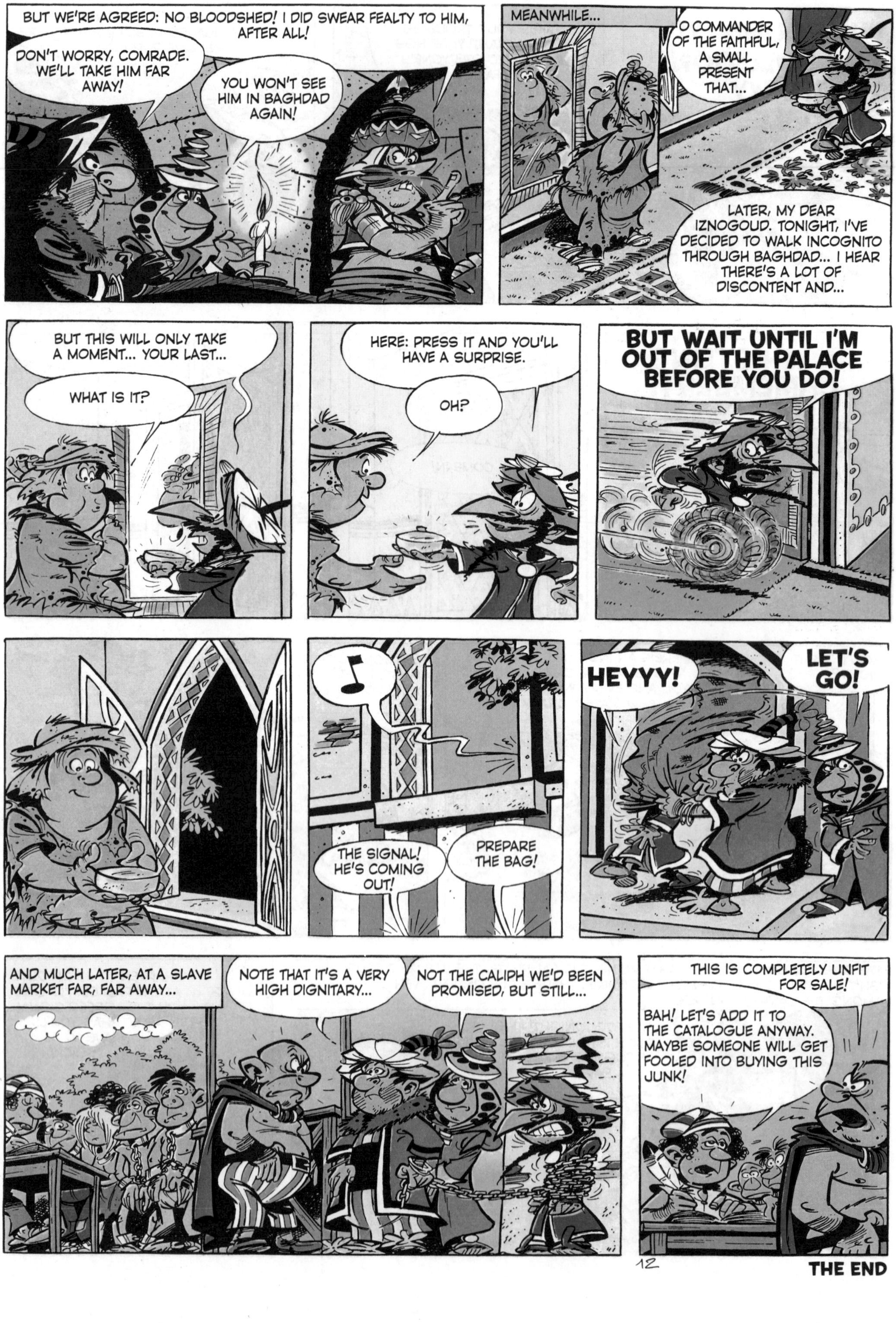

BUT WE'RE AGREED: NO BLOODSHED! I DID SWEAR FEALTY TO HIM, AFTER ALL!
DON'T WORRY, COMRADE. WE'LL TAKE HIM FAR AWAY!
YOU WON'T SEE HIM IN BAGHDAD AGAIN!
MEANWHILE...
O COMMANDER OF THE FAITHFUL, A SMALL PRESENT THAT...
LATER, MY DEAR IZNOGOUD. TONIGHT, I'VE DECIDED TO WALK INCOGNITO THROUGH BAGHDAD... I HEAR THERE'S A LOT OF DISCONTENT AND...
BUT THIS WILL ONLY TAKE A MOMENT... YOUR LAST...
WHAT IS IT?
HERE: PRESS IT AND YOU'LL HAVE A SURPRISE.
OH?
BUT WAIT UNTIL I'M OUT OF THE PALACE BEFORE YOU DO!
THE SIGNAL! HE'S COMING OUT!
PREPARE THE BAG!
HEYYY!
LET'S GO!
AND MUCH LATER, AT A SLAVE MARKET FAR, FAR AWAY...
NOTE THAT IT'S A VERY HIGH DIGNITARY...
NOT THE CALIPH WE'D BEEN PROMISED, BUT STILL...
THIS IS COMPLETELY UNFIT FOR SALE!
BAH! LET'S ADD IT TO THE CATALOGUE ANYWAY. MAYBE SOMEONE WILL GET FOOLED INTO BUYING THIS JUNK!
12

THE END